A Partridge in a Pear Tree

Twelve Days of Christmas

Emily E K Murdoch

ARE YOU SIGNED UP FOR DRAGONBLADE'S BLOG?

You'll get the latest news and information on exclusive giveaways, exclusive excerpts, coming releases, sales, free books, cover reveals and more.

Check out our complete list of authors, too!

No spam, no junk. That's a promise!

Sign Up Here

www.dragonbladepublishing.com

Dearest Reader;

Thank you for your support of a small press. At Dragonblade Publishing, we strive to bring you the highest quality Historical Romance from some of the best authors in the business. Without your support, there is no 'us', so we sincerely hope you adore these stories and find some new favorite authors along the way.

Happy Reading!

CEO, Dragonblade Publishing

Additional Dragonblade books by Author Emily E K Murdoch

Twelve Days of Christmas
Twelve Drummers Drumming
Eleven Pipers Piping
Ten Lords a Leaping
Nine Ladies Dancing
Eight Maids a Milking
Seven Swans a Swimming
Six Geese a Laying
Five Gold Rings
Four Calling Birds
Three French Hens
Two Turtle Doves
A Partridge in a Pear Tree

The De Petras Saga
The Misplaced Husband (Book 1)
The Impoverished Dowry (Book 2)
The Contrary Debutante (Book 3)
The Determined Mistress (Book 4)
The Convenient Engagement (Book 5)

The Governess Bureau Series
A Governess of Great Talents (Book 1)
A Governess of Discretion (Book 2)
A Governess of Many Languages (Book 3)
A Governess of Prodigious Skill (Book 4)
A Governess of Unusual Experience (Book 5)
A Governess of Wise Years (Book 6)
A Governess of No Fear (Novella)

Selina and Arthur and Dorothea
Caroline
Arabella
Sophia
Esther
Lucy
Jemima
London
Rupert and Frances
Joy
Harmony
William and Leonora
Olivia
Katarina
Isabella
Maria
Bath
Chalcroft
Fitzroy

CHAPTER ONE

"A H, SHE'S HERE!"

Isabella Fitzroy knew they would make a fuss. They always did, and it did not matter how much she attempted to fade into the background—her aunt, uncle, and two cousins beamed to see her.

"Isabella!" cried Harmony, her younger cousin seated by the fire.

Isabella smiled weakly. *Oh, all this attention.* She was sure she should be grateful, knew she was being uncharitable by hating the way her Bath relations fussed over her.

She had enough of that at home, at Chalcroft. All she wanted to do was come to Bath for the day, escape into the crowds, be a nobody in a sea of somebodies, then return home.

As it was...

Isabella forced a brave smile onto her face as her pelisse was removed by her aunt and her bonnet by a cousin.

"It really is too kind of you to invite me to visit," she said weakly, trying not to cringe at the way her family grew incredibly close, ignoring all sense of propriety and tucking a curl behind her ear. "Oh, thank you."

Did she really have to be treated like such a child? Isabella smiled awkwardly at Aunt Frances and Uncle Rupert, wishing to goodness they could just leave her alone.

It had been her mother's idea, of course. The moment Leonora heard her only unwed daughter was planning a day in Bath, she had hastily written to the Bath branch of the Fitzroy family and attempted to organize some sort of week for Isabella.

No matter how many times Isabella tried to stop her.

Well, she was determined this time. She was not going to be chaperoned and marched about by her family, she was not staying a week, and she was certainly not going to spend the entirety of the day here, sitting with her cousin Harmony rabbiting on without taking a breath.

"And how are the Chalcroft Fitzroys? How is Aunt Leonora? I suppose she is busy making the last of the presents for the servants—and Kitty, she is definitely coming to Chalcroft for Christmas?"

Laughter and chatter filled the drawing room as Isabella considered her escape.

The Bath Fitzroys lived relatively close to the center of town; once she was out of the house, it would not be long before she could slip into a crowd, unnoticed and unremarked upon.

Precisely what she wanted.

Isabella blinked at the onslaught of Harmony's words. She just needed a moment to think, a moment to be.

"Oh, what lovely hair you have," she said. A pitiful statement, she told herself. Rousing her nerves, she continued, "It is so elegant—is that the new style in Bath?"

"Oh, this?" Harmony laughed, patting her wayward hair. "No, this is just what my lady's maid can do with my hair in the five minutes before Rufus needs me! He is most charming, he— Here he is!"

A small boy covered in stickiness Isabella did not wish to encounter scampered into the room, a gingerbread man in each hand and crumbs all round his mouth.

"There's my grandson!" Uncle Rupert left Isabella's side and rushed toward Rufus, arms wide.

The child giggled raucously and rushed around the armchair,

and the room laughed.

Isabella smiled wryly. Well, it had been interesting while it lasted. That was the trouble with having three sisters, all with their own children, and goodness knew how many cousins with children of their own. It was impossible to last more than ten minutes without a child entering the room.

Not that she had anything against children—why, her nephews and nieces were some of the most precious children she had ever met!

Still. It would be pleasant, even for an hour, to merely be adults.

Her gaze caught that of her other cousin, Joy. The only unmarried Fitzroy other than herself—if the gossip from London about her cousin Sophia was true. Isabella saw the forced laugh, the way Joy tried to keep her feet out of the way of the unruly boy.

Perhaps she was not alone in this.

"Joy, will you not welcome our guest?" asked Aunt Frances pointedly.

Isabella's cheeks flushed with heat. They were not children anymore; she did not require her cousins to make a fuss of her when she came to visit. Quite to the contrary, she would rather prefer no fuss at all…

"Yes, of course," said Joy hastily, rising to her feet. "Wonderful to see you, Isabella."

Isabella kissed Joy's cheek. "Do not worry. I shall not keep you long."

She had whispered the words, certain Joy would understand her desire for quiet and anonymity in the crowds of Bath. After all, were they not cut from the same cloth?

"Now, sit down, Isabella, and we will get you some tea," said Aunt Frances distractedly as Harmony rushed off to attempt to catch her son. "Tea, tea… Ring the bell, will you, Joy?"

It was difficult not to smile, however, as Isabella watched Joy step over her nephew, around her father, and avoid tripping over

Harmony as she pulled the bell by the fireplace.

"I hope you do not mind the chaos—it comes with having children about the place," said Isabella's aunt with a laugh—a laugh that swiftly died as she looked into the eyes of Joy and Isabella.

Isabella swallowed. It was not that she minded, but really, the last thing she needed was for the family to draw constant attention to the fact that she was unmarried.

A few unpleasant, gossipy newspapers notwithstanding, she still had her reputation, her place in Society, her virtue—*not that any gentleman even wishes to take that*, she thought wryly—and a home in Chalcroft.

Truly, not every woman could be so lucky.

Isabella caught Joy's eye and saw the same pain. *Enough of this.* She was not going to permit herself to be treated like a martyr every time matrimony or babies were mentioned.

"Oh, do not worry about it, please," Isabella said softly, sitting down in an armchair as though she had not a care in the world. "You should see Chalcroft most of the time—absolutely *littered* with children!"

Did they hear the tension in her voice? Isabella was not entirely sure; Joy sat down without a word, and her uncle stood rather awkwardly by the fireplace.

She swallowed. She had to escape here, had to feel a little freedom before she returned to Chalcroft. It really was impossible to be alone there, save when in her bedchamber, and she did not wish to become that strange, spectral maiden aunt who kept to her rooms.

"Yes, how are your sisters?" asked Aunt Frances, her cheeks a little red as her husband and daughter rushed after Rufus, who knocked over a small console table. "They are well?"

Isabella smiled. "Very well, I thank you. They believe the improvements to Chalcroft Farm will be beneficial to the whole estate and, in the words of my sister Olivia, bring an element of elegance to the place."

Her aunt chuckled. "Olivia was always one to give herself airs."

Though she agreed, Isabella could not bring herself to say so. There was something about criticizing one's sister; to her face, absolutely, but with anyone else, even family? Never. There was an unspoken code of conduct there, one she would not break.

"I am so glad it is not snowing for your visit," said her aunt.

Isabella nodded. Goodness, to think how stilted some conversations were. "Yes, indeed. The weather is simply marvelous. We are fortunate the snow is not here yet, though I believe it will be soon. Don't you think?"

She had attempted to bring her cousin Joy into the conversation. There was nothing wrong with her aunt, of course, but it was strange being so examined, as though Aunt Frances was attempting to ascertain just how painful it was to be a single woman in the family.

But for some reason, Joy had not heard her. "I-I beg your pardon?"

"I said I think it is a marvelous day—the weather, I mean," said Isabella with a swift smile that just as swiftly disappeared. "I think I may go for a walk in town."

"Ah, what a shame we cannot accompany you!" said her aunt. "Your uncle and I have a prior engagement."

This was perfect. Isabella could not have hoped for anything better—now all she had to do was completely extricate herself from her cousins, too.

To be alone…a luxury at Chalcroft that she never managed.

Hoping they would not be offended, she raised her hand. "Please, do not apologize. After the noise and rush of Chalcroft, it would be pleasant to be…well, on my own, for an hour or two. I intend to return to Chalcroft this afternoon."

She saw her aunt and cousin exchange glances as Harmony lifted up her son by his ankles and the boy giggled raucously.

Isabella could see it in their eyes. They had received her mother's letter, had expected her to stay for several days, nearly a week. Why, it was only a week until Christmas; had they assumed they would be bringing her back to Chalcroft, where the entire Fitzroy family descended for the festive season?

Well, that would have to change. Isabella tried to keep her silence, knowing if she attempted to speak, she would talk herself out of it.

"Of course," said Aunt Frances finally, glancing at Joy. "You know the way."

Excitement rushed through Isabella as she rose to her feet. She was going to do it; she was going to escape the many Fitzroys and disappear off into Bath. To be anyone! Just a face in a crowd, not someone to be pitied.

"I do indeed." Isabella waited, expecting someone, any of them, to demand she be accompanied by a servant, a cousin, anyone. But nothing. She could not help but laugh. "You know, it is so strange. I truly did not believe you would permit me to walk on my own!"

Uncle Rupert shrugged as he rescued Harmony from her boy and popped him, still upside down, in an armchair. "You are old enough to know what is appropriate, Isabella, and you have been to Bath countless times. Do you believe you need a chaperone?"

"No," said Isabella with a smile.

Goodness, the last time she needed a chaperone… Well, it had been when the family believed she may actually marry. That was a long time ago.

Though it was odd, being given this freedom. She would just have to hope they would not write to her mother, nor tell her this Christmas, just what she had done.

"My father was terrified of my coming into town, but I must say, I feel a great deal more relaxed," admitted Isabella as she stepped to the door. "It was pleasant to see you all."

The door closed behind her. Isabella took a deep breath as she leaned against the door. She had done it. She had escaped the loving clutches of the Fitzroy family, and—

"Now what did…" began Joy through the door.

Isabella's heart skipped a beat. What were they talking about? Her?

There was nothing she hated more than gossip, and gossip about herself… Isabella swallowed, waiting, but heard nothing.

Well, there was no time like the present. There was no point waiting here when she could be enjoying the sights and sounds of the Season in Bath. Quickly pulling on the bonnet and pelisse that were removed from her so unwillingly, Isabella slipped out of the Fitzroy home, shut the door behind her, and breathed in deeply.

She was free.

Her feet naturally took her toward Milsom Street. This was where some of the most fashionable people could always be found, and Isabella adored standing there by a wall, watching the world go by.

So many colors, so many people. Faces chattering away excitedly; snatches of conversation caught on the wind. So much more than she could experience at Chalcroft.

Isabella's eyes followed a gentleman walking along Milsom Street with a rather fetching top hat with a feather in it—far too gauche for her liking, but fascinating nonetheless—and she was forced to look away hurriedly as he turned toward her.

She was not shy. Not really, not like her sister Maria.

But the last thing she wanted was to be discovered staring at a gentleman!

Isabella lifted her eyes, and to her horror saw the gentleman still staring—worse, he'd taken a step toward her, was approaching with a grin that could only be described as a leer.

"Oh Lord…" Isabella murmured, chest tightening.

Turning on her heels, she swiftly started walking in the opposite direction. Being an unmarried Fitzroy and claiming a little freedom was all very well, but she had no intention of speaking to a strange gentleman in the street!

Trying desperately not to give in to the temptation to turn and see if he was still following her, Isabella stepped down Green Street, a much quieter place with only a pair of ladies and a solitary gentleman walking toward her.

It happened suddenly, too suddenly for her to do anything. A man leapt out from a doorway, poorly dressed and without a hat, holding something that flashed in the wintry sun.

A knife. *A knife!*

Isabella froze, heart thumping wildly as panic rushed through her. A knife—she was about to be attacked. Oh, why had she not listened to her parents when they said walking in Bath on her own was too dangerous!

But it did not appear the man was interested in her. To the contrary, as the pair of ladies screamed and rushed backward, he approached the solitary gentleman.

Isabella reached out a hand and opened her mouth to cry out in warning, as though that could do any good. What on earth was she going to do? How could she—

But it appeared that she needn't have worried. The solitary gentleman looked up, saw the miscreant coming with a blade, and swiftly punched him.

The crack of the villain's nose breaking echoed down the street, and Isabella lifted a hand to her chest as she gasped. This was impossible! It could not be happening!

The man with the knife fell, groaning, clutching at his nose. The solitary gentleman, as though he often defended himself from attackers on the street and had no more interest in it than a card game, carefully trod on the man's hand, forcing him to release the knife.

Isabella leaned against a wall and tried to catch her breath, heart fluttering, cheeks flushed with panic and fear and...something else.

The gentleman straightened, and she saw, much to her disquiet, that the man was inordinately handsome. Tall, broad, a chiseled jawline the like of which she had never seen before, and his eyes...

Isabella swallowed. She was not supposed to find such violence...attractive. She was not supposed to be impressed by a gentleman who so swiftly used his fists.

But it was difficult not to be impressed.

"Go on with you," said the gentleman pleasantly, kicking away the knife. "Go on."

Still clutching his nose and leaving a trail of blood, the attacker half stumbled, half ran down the lane. He was gone in a moment. The quiet footsteps of the retreating pair of ladies disappeared, and the only sound left was Isabella's pulse in her ears.

They were alone. That was, she was alone with the gentleman who had so adeptly defended himself. Worse, he was looking at her.

Even worse—though Isabella could not help but think even better—he was smiling.

"I am sorry you had to witness that, miss," he said, stretching out his hand as though it too had been injured from the punch. "Not a pleasant sight."

Isabella swallowed, but the words in her mind slipped out before she could stop them. "I wouldn't say that."

Heat scalded her cheeks as he met her eyes. He was handsome—she could admit that to herself even if she never said it aloud.

Now there was a wry, lopsided smile on his face. "You do not look horrified."

Isabella drew herself up firmly. It was most outlandish to have this sort of bold conversation with a stranger, particularly one who had shown himself to be no stranger to violence.

She needed to leave, to escape this lane immediately and pretend what she had witnessed had never happened.

"I am," Isabella breathed, still leaning against the wall. "I am horrified."

The gentleman stepped toward her, and there was an intensity in his gaze as he said, "I am not sure you are. I think you rather enjoyed it."

Isabella's mouth fell open, but she was unable to refute his words. Why, wasn't her heart racing? Was she not drawn to him, a man so strong, so confident in his own abilities that he was swiftly able to reduce an attacker to a mess on the floor?

And it was ridiculous, Isabella knew, to feel such things. But that did not stop the feelings.

The gentleman was now just a foot from her, and he was still smiling, examining her boldly—far more boldly than any man ever had.

Isabella swallowed. She was not attracted to this gentleman, she told herself. Not in the slightest. She needed to escape him.

"I-I need to leave," she said.

The Fitzroy carriage had been left on Broad Street, and somehow Isabella managed to walk past the intriguing gentleman toward it—but he followed her, pushing through the crowds on the pavements of Bath to remain by her side.

"Far be it from me to abandon a lady in distress," he said cheerfully.

Isabella tried not to think about how close he was on the pavement to her, how close his hand was to hers, or just why he thought himself the appropriate person to walk with her.

As though…as though they were courting.

She pushed aside the thought. *Heaven forbid!*

"I am not in distress," she said sharply, reaching the carriage with relief. "Good day, sir."

Isabella had almost managed to get into the carriage on her own, but without a care in the world, without asking, without considering just what it would look like, he actually took her hand.

"Here, let me," he said in a low voice.

She could do nothing but permit him to help her into the carriage. As Isabella sat on the cushion inside, the gentleman leaned in, presumably to ascertain she was comfortably seated—and then he did it.

He kissed her.

Isabella gasped in his mouth. His lips were pressed firmly on hers, warm, passionate, eager, and she could do nothing but sit there and permit him to commit such an atrocity!

At least, that was what she was supposed to feel, she knew. But she did not feel violated, or scandalized, or outraged.

Oh no. She felt warm—desire rushed through her body as his lips worshipped hers; his tongue teased along her mouth, and just as she opened her lips, just as she welcomed him in, just as Isabella leaned forward to take advantage of every moment with him—

The kiss was over.

The gentleman grinned as he stepped back onto the pavement. "Well, well. Mr. Guy Partridge, at your service. We will meet again."

"What—"

Before Isabella could say another word, Mr. Partridge had shut the carriage door and slapped its side. The horses moved forward, pulling the carriage toward home—and Isabella was left to sit in shock.

CHAPTER TWO

THE CARRIAGE RIDE back to Chalcroft was a blur. Isabella's mind was entirely overtaken by the kiss she should not have given.

Not exactly *given*. As the carriage rattled along the country lanes, leaving the hustle and bustle of Bath behind, Isabella stared unseeing at the hedgerows covered with a dusting of frost, still unmelted in the weak December sun.

Not exactly *given*. It was taken from her, that kiss—her first kiss—but she could not despise the man for doing it.

Why, the way he touched her...the power of his lips, the way he seemed to know precisely how she wanted to be kissed—which was madness. She had never been kissed before—she herself did not know!

"Well, well. Mr. Guy Partridge, at your service. We will meet again."

Isabella swallowed, unable to push the image of Mr. Partridge from her mind. The tall man, the way he effortlessly defended himself, the power of his hands...hands that had helped her into the Fitzroy carriage just before he kissed her...

"I am horrified."

"I am not sure you are. I think you rather enjoyed it."

Isabella shivered as the carriage came to a stop outside Chalcroft. She had certainly been aroused by his power in a way she had never experienced before.

Oh, there were plenty of pleasant enough gentlemen in her acquaintance. That was, her family's acquaintance. The Fitzroy family was one to be courted, she well knew, and there were many neighbors with which they were on good terms.

Even her brothers-in-law were perfectly pleasant enough, most of the time. She was still becoming acclimatized, in truth, to the addition of Walter to the family, but then, she was biased. He was the one who had allowed slander of her name to be published in the newspapers a few years ago.

But Guy—Mr. Partridge—was nothing like them.

No, she did not warm in their presence as she did with him. She was not impressed by the way they held themselves, as she could not drag her eyes away from Guy. She did not—

"Miss Fitzroy?"

Isabella blinked. The carriage door had been opened, utterly unbeknownst to her, and their driver was waiting patiently for her to take his hand and step out of the carriage.

She smiled weakly. "Ah, thank you."

It was impossible not to notice that when she took her driver's hand, it was nothing like Guy's. When Guy had taken her hand, most unexpectedly and, in truth, entirely rebelliously, for they had not been formally introduced—why, she had not even known his name at the time—her whole chest warmed, and a rush of something she did not understand overtook her body.

But here, now, it was nothing more than the simple habit of a servant.

Isabella straightened up on the Chalcroft drive and smiled at her home. *Chalcroft.* A majestic home, her father called it. Falling apart, her mother would mutter, her Italian blood seething at the rising costs of keeping the place warm.

Isabella had known no other home, and unless her fortunes changed, she never would.

"Well, well. Mr. Guy Partridge, at your service. We will meet again."

Isabella squared her shoulders and walked toward the front door. No, she would not give this Guy Partridge any more of her time, nor her thoughts. He did not deserve them. Who was he but a gentleman—more ruffian, in truth—who managed his fists just as well as his lips?

"Ah, there you are!"

It was with a weary smile that Isabella saw her mother. "I said I would not be gone long."

"But I was given to understand you would be spending a few days with your uncle Rupert," said Leonora distractedly, as a gaggle of grandchildren rushed by. "I thought—"

"No, you *hoped*," said Isabella wryly, removing her bonnet and wishing to goodness it was possible to have a conversation without all her nieces and nephews about the place.

Not that it would change much. Her mother still considered her with the same sort of approach as the little ones. Once a child, always a child, clearly.

"But I told your aunt Frances—"

"I knew they looked at me strangely when I said I was only visiting for the day," said Isabella ruefully, removing her pelisse and turning to glare at her mother. "You really must listen to me, Mama. I told you before I left—"

"Put that down, Tommy, or I will tan your hide so hard you will never sit down again," said Leonora, rushing away from her daughter.

Isabella had to smile as she watched her eldest nephew very carefully replace the heavy golden clock he had attempted to walk off with.

"Do not mind me, Mama," she said softly under her breath as her mother was distracted by another errant child. "I'll just stand here, growing older and older, with no opportunity to experience my own life, my own independence…"

It was not fair, really, to be so bitter. Most of the time Isabella was perfectly happy at Chalcroft: wandering through the woodlands, helping out on the farm, reading by the fire, playing the pianoforte very poorly—even she had to admit it.

It was only at this time of year when she was reminded just how much her sisters' lives had continued on without her, and she had just…remained. Exactly as she had been when she first entered Society.

"Dinner is whenever you wish it," called out her mother from the next room, evidently not considering her daughter important enough to return to the hall. "It's just whatever you can find in the kitchen, nothing special."

Nothing special. Isabella forced a smile and tried not to take it to heart. No, nothing special. That would do for Isabella; God forbid she enjoy anything special.

Like the kiss that had been stolen from her just an hour before…

Cheeks hot, burning with the embarrassment both of the kiss and how much she had enjoyed it, Isabella turned to the staircase. Her appetite was gone. All she could think about was Guy.

Mr. Partridge, she told herself sternly as she reached the landing and wandered down the corridor to her bedchamber. It was outrageous to be thinking of him in such a way!

Almost as outrageous as what he had done to her…

Isabella closed her bedchamber door and leaned on it, closing her eyes. She had never imagined, when she left this room earlier today, that she would go into Bath, witness a violent attack on a stranger, watch that stranger deal with the situation with ease, and then…

And then…

"Well, well. Mr. Guy Partridge, at your service. We will meet again."

Isabella swallowed. She was an innocent in theory, but she knew of the practice, knew what a man and a woman could share with each other. She was not ignorant of how her nieces and nephews came into being.

Never before had she considered such a thing may happen to her. Isabella was well aware her family considered her the old maid, the maiden aunt, the Fitzroy that was too shy, too quiet, too enclosed in Chalcroft to meet someone who may have a passing interest in her.

And perhaps that was all this was: a passing fancy. Isabella opened her eyes and heaved a great sigh. Perhaps Guy—perhaps Mr. Partridge kissed ladies all the time. Perhaps this was all par for the course for him, and though it was special to her, it was nothing but a cold, wintry December day for him.

It was not a pleasant thought.

Unwilling to descend once more into the depths of Chalcroft and put up with her parents' questions about what she did in Bath that day—none of which Isabella believed she could answer honestly—she pulled off her gown, allowing it to fall in a heap on the floor, pulled on her favorite winter nightgown, made of thick wool, and clambered into bed.

Sometimes there was nothing for it but to sleep.

"Well, well. Mr. Guy Partridge, at your service. We will meet again. In fact, why don't I stay now and show you just how I like to be kissed..."

Isabella knew it was a dream. There was no possibility this was real: this closeness, this intensity, Guy's arms around her waist and his lips once more on hers. But she did not care. What did it matter if it was a dream?

Here, in her imagination, it did not matter if Guy was real, whether these kisses would ever truly mean something, whether he had good intentions or ill. She luxuriated in the dream, her senses overwhelmed by imagined kisses trailing down her neck.

"Guy..." she moaned.

Oh, it was too much. This desire in her, desire never unlocked before, was pouring from her like from a broken dam—and yet not from her heart.

No, that was not where this sensual dream was taking her, and though Isabella knew it to be wrong, knew that young ladies should certainly not be thinking or feeling anything of the sort...what was the harm?

The dream Guy broke the kiss, smiling, and started to remove her gown. Isabella let him, eyelashes fluttering as his fingers scraped across her skin.

"Guy…"

"Isabella," whispered the dream Guy, allowing her gown to fall to the floor.

And Isabella felt no embarrassment—why should she? This was right, this was perfect, and, best of all, this was a dream no one else would ever discover. She could explore here, taste here, feel everything she wanted to…

"Isabella?"

Isabella turned slightly in her dream. The man before her had not spoken—could not speak, for his lips were trailing kisses from her wrist to her elbow. But she had definitely heard her name spoken.

"Isabella Fitzroy."

There it was again. Despite herself, Isabella slowly wrenched herself from the delightful dream she was basking in and found, to her surprise, she had placed her hand between her legs. Her secret place was throbbing, aching, needing something she could not give it.

And that was not the only surprising thing. She was not alone.

"Isabella Fitzroy, my word," whispered Guy Partridge, sitting on her windowsill. "I never would have guessed."

Isabella started, heart racing, lungs tight, nausea rushing through her stomach. She hastily removed her hand from her secret place, hoping to goodness he had not seen what she…

Guy grinned. "Hello."

Isabella blinked. She propped herself up against her pillows, yet the image of Guy Partridge appeared once more in her vision.

Guy—Guy in her bedchamber? What on earth was he doing here?

Her instincts overtook her, and Isabella opened her mouth to scream, to declare danger, to shout that there was an intruder in the house.

"Peace," he said softly, rising from the windowsill and stepping quietly toward her. "I mean you no harm."

Isabella hesitated for a moment, gaze fixed upon the man who certainly could not be here—it was impossible that he was here. Was this a dream still? Had it merely changed, rather than disappeared entirely?

A heavy weight sank at the end of her bed. Guy Partridge had helped himself to a corner of her mattress. Isabella could feel the bed move under his pressure.

So. This was not a dream—or, at least, it was the most realistic dream she'd had in a long time. Other than...

Flames seared her cheeks as Isabella realized what Guy had undoubtedly witnessed her doing. Touching herself while dreaming of him...for all she knew, she had cried out his name, just as she had in the dream!

Oh, this was a nightmare! And worst of all, there was a stranger in her bedchamber—a strange gentleman. A gentleman she barely knew, but had kissed. This was not going to be something she could explain to her family in the morning...

Isabella swallowed, heart still racing. "What are you doing here?"

That lopsided grin she already knew so well appeared on his face, and he tilted his head as he had done when questioning her in the lane.

"I think you rather enjoyed it."

"What am I doing here?" he said quietly. "You think I would kiss a woman, enjoy it so much, then never see her again?"

Isabella stared. This was absolutely scandalous—if she heard, or more likely read in a gossip sheet, that a gentleman had been found in a lady's bedchamber, she would of course assume the absolute worst.

Forcing aside the memories of the dream she had been indulging in, Isabella whispered, "But...but you are here."

It did not make sense. It was the most exciting thing that had ever happened. Though she knew it was impossible for him to stay, Isabella ached to have him closer. To know his touch. To feel his kiss again, just once. Just once, that was all.

"How…how did you know me?" she whispered. "How did you know where I was?"

It was inexplicable, his presence here. Isabella's heart was still pacing wildly, and it skipped a beat as Guy smiled.

"Oh, that was simple," he said easily in a low voice. "I merely asked everyone in Bath who the most beautiful woman in the world was, and they sent me here."

She laughed at that. Well, what woman did not want to hear such pleasantries?

In the darkness of the night, Guy shook his head wryly. "That, or I saw the livery on your carriage and enquired as to the location of the Fitzroy home. It was not difficult to find."

Isabella smiled, pushing herself upright to look directly at him. Only then did she remember she was wearing naught but a nightgown. Heat searing through her chest, she pulled up the blanket to greater protect her, but as Guy was seated on the bed, that was impossible.

"If…if you would not mind," she managed to say.

"In fact, I do mind," said Guy quietly. "I mind very much indeed. I rather like the view I have, you see."

Isabella dropped her gaze immediately. How could he say such a thing? How could he think such things, let alone say them?

But Guy did not seem to have any trouble with saying the thoughts in his mind, an attribute she had to admire. It was not one they shared, and everything about this experience was tantalizingly different from the whole of her life.

"But why?" she breathed, unable to look at him. "Why…why seek me out?"

The question had poured from her lips before she could censor herself, and in those heart-stopping moments afterward, Isabella wished she had.

What a wanton thing to say! Why could she not just be flattered that Guy Partridge had wished to see her at all?

But Guy did not censure her. To the contrary, he moved forward, along the bed, and Isabella could only gasp as he lifted her chin with a finger, forcing her to look into his eyes.

"Why do you think?" he asked softly.

Isabella stared. This was unlike anything she had known, anything she had expected.

A gentleman—a stranger!—in her bedchamber, a man she only met a few hours ago and had already stolen a kiss from, now seated on her bed, touching her…touching her so gently and softly, with a reverence she did not understand.

Because it did not match his eyes. No, in Guy's eyes was fiery desire, a passion she could not understand but could feel throbbing between her legs.

"I…I think…" Isabella said. What did she think? How could she think, with Guy just inches away from her now?

She was practically in bed with a man!

"I think I want to know how you got into my bedchamber," she said softly.

Guy grinned. "I climbed up the pear tree, of course."

Isabella shifted her gaze from him to the window behind him. Yes, the pear tree. Far too large for that side of the house, her mother had always said, and it only gave a few pears each season, but she loved it. A canopy of leaves right outside her bedchamber.

A route in for marauding gentleman.

"You…you cannot be here."

Guy raised an eyebrow. "Are you saying that you want me to go?"

Isabella's heart ached. The idea of Guy leaving, of disappearing, of whatever this was ending so quickly—it was anathema to her. She did not want him to go.

But she could hardly admit such a thing, could she?

"No," she breathed.

Guy's eyes darkened, just for a moment, and he blew out a breath slowly. "Oh, Miss Isabella Fitzroy. You are most definitely not what I expected."

"But you cannot kiss me again," Isabella said hastily.

He laughed quietly. "You did not like my kiss?"

"No, it's just—"

"So you *did* like my kiss?"

Isabella swallowed. This was getting out of hand—far too out of hand. "You really should not be here."

"And yet I am," said Guy, his fierce gaze not leaving hers. "Here I am, Isabella, and I want to be here, and so do you. I won't touch you, you don't have to be afraid of that, though I sorely wish to."

Isabella gasped, her whole body tingling at the mere suggestion.

"So why don't we…talk?"

"Talk?" she repeated weakly. She could think of nothing to say, no questions to ask, not while her whole body was entranced by Mr. Guy Partridge.

Guy grinned. "Talk."

CHAPTER THREE

I SABELLA WAS NOT one typically to complain. At least, not aloud. Many times she had railed against the decisions of her parents but, like a good daughter, rarely voiced it.

Now, however, she wished she had voiced it earlier.

"But I have no wish to dine with the neighbors," she said quietly as the carriage rattled along the lane. "I could just as easily have stayed home with—"

"Nonsense," said her mother.

Isabella smiled wryly. Leonora Fitzroy was not a woman to be crossed by anyone, let alone one of her daughters. It was a rare person indeed who felt bold enough to go against her mother's wishes.

Still, it was tiring to the extreme to be trotted out with her parents whenever they received an invitation to dine. In truth, Isabella was rarely included on the invitations. There had been a few awkward situations when a place was not laid for her, as *she* had not actually been invited.

But this evening, just five days before Christmas, Isabella could not deny her name had been carefully written on the note sent to her mother, so the three of them had been bundled into a carriage to disappear off for dinner.

Isabella sighed as the carriage rattled along, jolting her against the window. It was most irritating—all the more so because it had prevented her from going into Bath that day.

"Bath?" Her father had blinked at her only that morning. "Why on earth do you want to go to Bath? You went yesterday."

And Isabella had been forced to smile, nod, and agree she had been in Bath yesterday.

"Here I am, Isabella, and I want to be here, and so do you. I won't touch you, you don't have to be afraid of that, though I sorely wish to."

She swallowed and tried not to think about the conversation she had shared with Guy Partridge into the early hours of the night. A conversation about music, art, science. About the politics of the wars in France, about why the weather was so ill this time of year.

Anything, in short, to avoid the topic that she wished to speak on.

Why, oh why, had he come to her bedchamber?

Isabella sighed. *Guy Partridge.* She knew nothing of him, had not had the confidence to ask her father whether he had ever heard the name. For all she knew, he was an absolute brigand, a man not to be trusted.

Really, had he not given her enough proof of his unsuitability? Punching a man in the street, kissing her in the carriage, appearing in her bedchamber…

It was absolutely outrageous.

A smile crept across Isabella's mouth.

And delicious, there was no doubt about it.

"Here we are," said William Fitzroy eagerly.

Isabella glanced at her father and tried not to laugh. He hated carriages. Perhaps that was why her branch of the Fitzroy family so rarely went to Town, or to Bath. It was all her father could do to manage a twenty-minute carriage journey to their nearest neighbor.

"And not before time, too," Isabella said. "Else I believe your luncheon would have been coating our skirts."

She caught her mother's eye, and they both grinned.

"Welcome, welcome!" said Lord Jellicoe as they stepped into

the hall. "So wonderful to see you again—my word, Miss Fitzroy, you do not look a day older."

Isabella tried to fix a smile on her face. Why was it that whenever she met with anyone, they had to remark on how young she was looking?

As though she was not perfectly aware that she was aging, just as everyone else was. Really, one of these days she would have to say something—if she could bring herself to.

But she merely smiled, curtseyed, and wished to goodness the evening was over already. After all, it was not as though there would be anyone to capture her attention—

"Ah, Mr. Partridge, meet my neighbors, the Fitzroys," said Lord Jellicoe eagerly.

Isabella froze in the middle of giving her pelisse to a footman. *No*. It wasn't possible. Partridge was perhaps a common name, but not that common…

Guy Partridge stepped through from the drawing room and beamed at the Fitzroys before him. "Mr. Fitzroy, Mrs. Fitzroy…Miss Fitzroy."

He inclined his head to each of them in turn, giving Isabella plenty of time to compose herself and rearrange her face into an uninterested and genteel expression.

At least, that was what she had intended. In truth, when Guy bowed with that knowing grin on his face, all Isabella could do was stammer and flush, her cheeks painfully hot.

"Mr. Partridge," murmured her mother, curtseying.

Just in time, Isabella remembered to follow suit. The last thing she wanted was for her hosts—or God forbid, her parents—to believe there was something the matter with her. How would she explain this particular secret?

"Yes, my friend Partridge here is a true benefactor to the poor," continued Lord Jellicoe, gesturing that they should all go into the drawing room. "A better man I have never met, though his billiards certainly leaves something to be desired…"

Isabella allowed herself to be pulled through into the drawing room, seating herself on a sofa, and was pleased but unsurprised when Guy sat beside her.

"Benefactor to the poor?" she repeated under her breath, not quite having the bravery to look at him as she spoke.

At least her parents seemed uninterested in the sudden appearance of a stranger in their midst. They were too preoccupied with speaking with Lord Jellicoe about boundaries, the terrible ruffians one saw on the roads these days, and, of course, grandchildren.

Isabella sighed. *Of course.*

"I am sorry, are you talking to me?"

She looked up in surprise at Guy, who was grinning. "Of course I was talking to you."

"Ah," he said, his smile becoming teasing. "I was not sure, you see, for you were not looking at me. Am I so hideous that you cannot bear the sight of me?"

Isabella flushed. He knew perfectly well, she was certain, that he was a remarkably handsome man, one any lady would take pleasure in looking at. She was not going to give him the satisfaction of knowing it.

At least, she would not say it. Her cheeks were definitely giving her away.

"I said, benefactor to the poor?" she repeated, doing her best to hold his gaze and hating the way he made her entire body quiver just with a look. "You did not mention that last ni—at our last meeting."

Had her parents heard? Isabella glanced across to them seated by the fire with Lord Jellicoe, and saw to her relief they were far too involved in their conversation to listen to hers.

"Old Jellicoe's words, not mine," said Guy easily. "But they are true."

"I must commend you, I suppose, for doing so much for the less fortunate."

Yes, that was it: stay on safe topics, like the weather, and charity, and the poor. That way she could force from her mind the images of the Guy she already knew far too well—the handsome man kissing her in the carriage, the dashing, debonair man sitting on the edge of her bed, just fingertips away, the rogue climbing down her pear tree…

"Well, once you have been one of the less fortunate," Guy said quietly, not taking his eyes from hers, "you start to realize just how important that help can be."

Isabella stared. It was astonishing to hear him speak so calmly, so eloquently about being one of the less fortunate. Did he mean… Why, he was attired in the garb of a gentleman. In every moment she had been with him, Guy held himself in the posture of a gentleman—a rake, true, but a rakish *gentleman*, nonetheless.

Heat tinged her cheeks, but Isabella leaned forward. He was intriguing, this man who thought it acceptable to clamber into a lady's bedchambers and not seduce her.

Not that she wished him to. Obviously.

An image from her rather erotic dream tripped into her mind, and Isabella did her best to push it away. She was not going to lose her head!

"Tell me about it," she said quietly. "Tell me about yourself. We spoke on so much yester—before, but nothing about yourself."

Guy raised a quizzical eyebrow. "Are you saying you wish to know me better?"

Isabella swallowed. She wished to know him better than was appropriate, though she could say no such thing.

She was a Fitzroy, with a prim and proper reputation, she knew. Only occasionally did Isabella wish she could throw it to the winds and embark on a ridiculous love affair.

Oh, to know what it was to be touched, to be kissed, to be worshipped—for pleasure to be the only currency worth holding—

"Miss Fitzroy?"

"What?" Isabella said distractedly.

She blinked. Lord Jellicoe's drawing room came back into

focus—as did Guy.

He was grinning. "You're thinking about me, aren't you?"

"No," said Isabella hastily. "I mean, yes. Not like that."

Guy's grin widened. "Like what?"

"Nothing." *Blast the man!* "You were going to tell me about yourself."

For a moment, she was certain he would refuse. It was a rather personal query, after all, and they had only in the last few minutes been formally introduced.

Not that it had prevented her from technically having him in her bed…

"Oh, I wish I could peer into that mind of yours, Isabella Fitzroy," Guy said, his voice low. "But as it is… Well."

He cleared his throat, and Isabella glanced once more at her parents. They seemed absolutely unperturbed that she was seated alone with a strange gentleman—but then, they had no idea that she had any sort of prior acquaintance with Guy.

Acquaintance. A strange sort of word to encapsulate what they had shared…

"Well, there is not much to tell, not really," said Guy, leaning back on the sofa but leaving his hands by his sides. Close to her. "My father was a good man, though not a particularly clever one, and a few bad decisions and conversations with men of ill repute meant he fell from grace. He died shortly afterward."

Compassion rushed through Isabella's heart, mingling with the desire that Guy's mere presence sparked in her. A sorry tale indeed.

"It was therefore my responsibility, as the son, to work hard and build up the family name again, something I have dedicated the better portion of my life to," said Guy. "Though now I think about it, I must consider that that particular job is never done."

Isabella smiled weakly. "No. No, I suppose not."

He had suffered, then. Though there was a sparkle of mischief in his eyes, though he stole kisses from her—well, one kiss— he had known true difficulty.

Far more than she had ever endured, Isabella thought ruefully. She knew of such things from books, from the newspapers, from the conversations of others. Not in her life.

"It must take a great deal of strength and character," she found herself saying quietly, "to raise one's family after such tragedy."

Guy nodded sagely. "I suppose so. But I suppose I should not be saying such things to a beautiful woman, at a dinner party."

Isabella flushed. "You should not?"

He was close. Had he moved? She had no recollection of him doing any such thing, yet she was certain he was closer now. Why, their hands were almost touching.

If she just leaned ever so slightly…

"Particularly a Fitzroy," said Guy softly, his eyes not leaving hers. "Especially not a woman so beautiful, so radiant. So easily able to spark in me a desire I have never—"

"Hush!" Isabella said.

Heart beating painfully, she glanced around. More dinner guests of Lord Jellicoe had arrived but were congregated far from them. It was not possible they had heard him.

Such nonsense, she told herself. *Such flattery.*

Though now she looked at Guy, nervously through her lashes, Isabella was certain she could see evidence of…well, desire. As though he greatly wished to kiss her, something she would welcome.

At least, if she was not seated here in a room full of people.

Isabella swallowed as Guy moved another inch closer. "You shouldn't."

"I know," he said quietly, moving his hand closer to hers. "And yet here I am."

This was not happening. It simply did not happen to ladies such as her! Isabella could not recall a single gentleman ever showing more than a passing interest in her. The idea of a gentleman being attracted to her was unheard of.

And yet here he was. Guy Partridge. The most handsome

man she had ever seen, sitting now only an inch away from her.

His fingers brushed up against hers, and Isabella gasped. The intensity, the pleasure that rippled through her, the frisson that rushed up her spine at the forbidden touch.

Her mind was immediately reminded of the kiss—that kiss, their only kiss, but what a kiss. A kiss that took the very best of her yet gave something even sweeter in return. A kiss that riled her up so much she had…touched herself that very evening.

Touched herself while she dreamt of him touching her…

"You are thinking about kissing me."

Isabella stared, brushing her hand past Guy's as he looked at her intensely. "I'm not."

Well, it was not precisely a lie. Even as her cheeks filled with heat and her lungs tightened, every breath becoming more difficult, Isabella knew she had not lied.

At least, she had not been imagining that Guy was kissing her on the lips…

"You are," murmured Guy, and he took her hands in his own. "You are thinking about kissing me. About my lips on yours, raining heat down your neck as I long to reach your breasts, but I don't. I return to your mouth, plundering it for pleasure, giving far more than I take."

Isabella could not breathe. He could not be saying such things to her, such things that made her warm, made her whole body ache for him…made her secret place throb…

"And I am thinking about kissing you," Guy continued, his dark eyes flashing as he smiled wickedly. "I am thinking about kissing you all over, Isabella. All over. Even there."

She gasped, trying to mute it as best she could but struggling to contain herself. She knew precisely where he meant; he did not need to say it.

How could he see right into her mind, into her desires, into those forbidden parts of herself that she had refused to ever consider until she met him? He was dangerous, this man, and yet she wanted nothing more than to be alone with him.

Alone with him for hours…

"How can you say such things?" she asked.

Guy swallowed, and just for a moment, she saw a meager amount of uncertainty. And then it was gone, and his confident smile returned. "Because you are, and you should. That kiss, Isabella…oh, that kiss was the best I ever had."

She could feel his pulse in his fingers as he held her hand—or was that her own pulse, quick, and throbbing, and mirroring the growing ache in her?

"And if all these people were not here," whispered Guy, his voice just louder than a breath, "I would kiss you right here. I would kiss you here until you begged for mercy."

"I never beg," she breathed.

Guy groaned quietly. "Oh, I will make you pay for saying that. Isabella—"

A gong rang in the hall. He dropped her hand immediately. The crowd of guests at the other end of the room turned and made their preparations to go into the dining room.

Isabella could barely breathe. How would she rise to her feet and walk sedately through with them, as though nothing had happened? As though she hadn't had scalding words of seduction murmured in her ear.

"Miss Fitzroy?"

She looked up. Guy was standing, offering his hand, a mischievous smile on his face.

She had no intention of taking his hand, none whatsoever. It was most infuriating, therefore, that Isabella did so immediately without thinking.

Any opportunity to touch Guy, to be touched by him, was an opportunity she did not wish to waste.

"I say again, that kiss yesterday was the best I ever had," Guy whispered as he pulled her ever so slightly closer to him than was necessary. "And I will not rest, Isabella Fitzroy, until I taste you again."

CHAPTER FOUR

WHEN ISABELLA HEARD a noise that night as she lay in bed, absolutely, definitely not thinking about Guy Partridge, a small smile crept over her face.

She knew that noise. It was a relatively new one in her life, but she had already attuned her ear to that sound. A scraping, a muttering, and the movement of branches just outside her bedchamber door.

There was only one thing that could be. One person.

Only one man was so bold as to climb up her pear tree and attempt to gain access to her bedchamber through her window.

Her heart pattered painfully in her chest as Isabella sat up in bed. Was it him? Who else could it be? After such a delicious time talking with him at Lord Jellicoe's dinner, she'd found her mind utterly swept with thoughts of Guy—Mr. Partridge, as she should call him—and it seemed almost too good to be true that he was visiting her illicitly once more.

But surely it could not be anyone else…

A sudden low thud and a muttered curse echoed through her bedchamber, and Isabella stifled a laugh. Well, he was evidently not as adept at climbing up trees as he made out last time he visited.

Swallowing, knowing she should not be giving herself the opportunity to be discovered in such a scandalous position,

Isabella found it was impossible to stay within her warm bed.

She crept out from under the covers, slipped on her robe, and stepped across the dark room toward the window, which was hidden by the heavy curtain.

Isabella reached out to pull it open, then hesitated. If she did no more, she could claim innocence if the sudden appearance of a man in her bedchamber was discovered. If she opened the curtains, however, she would be able to claim no such thing.

This was her last chance to pretend she did not know what was occurring.

Isabella's heart pattered in her chest, increasing in pace with every second she stood there, hand hanging in the air indecisively. Did she want an adventure with a stranger?

Though in truth, Guy—Mr. Partridge; she really must try to remember!—had told her much about his family just a few hours ago. How many other gentlemen had she spoken to so openly?

And did she not want to see him? Did she not ache in the absence of him, the memory of that kiss he stole just days ago?

Isabella's hand moved of its own accord. The curtain opened.

There, on the other side of the glass, was Guy Partridge.

She stifled a grin. Truly, it was most wanton! But she had done nothing wrong; it was hardly her fault if gentlemen were climbing up to her window to whisper sweet nothings.

Not that he would do so, Isabella told herself firmly. No, that was nonsense. Besides, he could not do so, not with the window closed again him.

It took just a small amount of effort to push up the window and prop up the sash.

"Why, hello there," said Guy in a low, sensuous voice. "Do you come here often?"

Isabella melted. She very nearly lost all control of her legs, and it was a relief to gently collapse onto the wide window seat.

How did he do it? Why did Guy's voice reach something deep and dark within her, changing her, allowing her body to quiver at the promise of pleasure that lay within his tone?

She had never met anyone like him. Never.

"I rather think I should be asking you that same question," Isabella said quietly, relieved her voice sounded calm, even if her heart was not. "I mean, for all I know, you have been climbing up my pear tree for months to spy on me."

The thought was delicious, and she tried not to think about it. The idea she may have undressed before this very window, assuming no one could possibly see her, but Guy was hiding there, in the branches, hidden by the leaves…

Warmth pooled between her legs, but Isabella resolutely ignored it. She would not permit herself to give in.

"You know, I wish I had been frequenting this rather delightful pear tree and looking at you, Isabella," said Guy quietly, settling himself on the windowsill and examining her closely. "And I think you would like that, wouldn't you? You like to be watched."

Isabella flushed and looked down at her hands clasped tightly in her lap, and tried not to think about how she had touched herself just a night ago with Guy watching.

She had not known, of course—and would certainly not have done so if she had.

Or would she? There was, she had to admit, something rather glorious in the idea that as she was touching herself, exploring herself, he was there watching, eagerly taking in the sight of her…perhaps learning how she wanted to be touched…

Isabella swallowed. As she looked up, Guy was still looking at her, unashamed, as though this topic of conversation was perfectly natural and, if anything, to be expected.

"What have you come here for?"

Guy raised an eyebrow, as though the answer was obvious. "Why, you, of course."

It's the cool night air, Isabella told herself. That was the reason why her skin tingled. It was nothing to do with the idea that Guy desired her, as she desired him.

No one desired her; she had learnt that long ago—had learnt

to expect nothing from the few gentlemen she encountered throughout the year.

But this Guy…he was something different. Something entirely unique.

"Me?" Isabella breathed.

Guy grinned. "You think I did not see the way you looked at me at dinner? My word, Isabella Fitzroy, I rather thought if we had been left alone that you would eat me up."

"I certainly would do no such thing!" Isabella protested, ignoring the intrigue his words sparked in her heart.

"What a shame," came the shameless reply. "I would rather like to eat you up."

This was not happening. This had to be a dream—though how she had dreamt up such scandalous things to put in Guy's mouth, she could not conceive!

But it was surely not possible that such a man, so handsome, so kind to the poor, so resolutely real, was here, desiring her, speaking to her in such a way. Why, there was almost a moan in his words just then, as though he truly desired her.

As though, given half the chance, he would follow through on his words…

Isabella tried to examine the face of the man before her, but though a half-moon illuminated the gardens and grounds, there was something unknowable in Guy's expression.

"Well, I hope you ate your fill at Lord Jellicoe's, for I am afraid you will receive little sustenance here," she said as lightly as she could manage. "And if you expected to be let in, I can assure you, I will be doing no such thing."

"Oh, Isabella, you break my heart," said Guy with a wheedling smile. He shifted along the window seat. "Is there anything I can say to change your mind?"

Yes, thought Isabella. *Oh, God, yes.* "No."

"Are you sure?" Guy's smile did not disappear, not exactly, but it changed. There was a wicked, hungry look about it now that made Isabella's stomach twist. "I beg you, Isabella. I crave you. I need you. The way your eyes look at me make me want to do desperate things, for being apart from you, even this small distance, is hurting me…"

His voice faded into a whisper, and Isabella found she could not look away.

And why would she? It was intensely…well, *erotic* was the only word she could think of. There was no other way to describe it. The way he looked at her, his pleading tone, the way her whole body was heating up despite the December chill.

Oh, to be so desired, it was heady, making her giddy.

"You…you are very persuasive, Mr. Partridge," she managed.

Guy shifted another inch closer. "Mr. Partridge? Oh, Isabella, I would have thought we would be on first-name terms by now. After all, I know the taste of your mouth."

"Guy!"

That wicked smile danced about his mouth. "Don't tell me you don't like it."

Isabella opened her mouth to say that she certainly did *not* like it, and would not permit him to say such things.

But she could not. Not while Guy's gaze drifted to her open mouth, lust sparked in his eyes, and a slow moan emanated from his lips.

"Isabella, you don't know what you do to me…"

This was nonsense, Isabella attempted to tell herself as she closed her mouth and swallowed, not once but twice. He was a man accustomed to flirting, he must be, so she could not trust nor believe a single word he said. No, she would need to force him into a little more honesty before she could let him—

Not that she was going to let him do anything!

"Guy Partridge, I do not believe a word you say," Isabella managed, with a small laugh. "And I am certainly not going to let you into my bedchamber. Not until—"

"Until?" he cut in eagerly.

A strange feeling twisted around her heart. She had power here. It was odd; she had never had power over anyone before, let alone a handsome gentleman begging her for…her.

"Until you tell me something true," Isabella finished.

She had expected Guy to be a little bashful, but she should not have been surprised by his almost immediate grin.

"Why, that is simple," he said. "You taste sweeter than any pear."

Heat scalded Isabella's cheeks. He was outrageous!

And he was fast becoming the only person Isabella wanted to talk to, all day.

"No," she replied. "I said something true."

"It is true," Guy said with a grin. "Though you are right—it has been some time since I was gifted with the pleasure of your mouth. Here, let me taste again."

He leaned forward, his nose grazing her own, and was just about to steal another kiss when Isabella moved back.

It was only an inch, but it was enough.

Guy groaned as he sat upright again. "You tease, Isabella."

Isabella tried to catch her breath. That had been close—and not close enough. She was not sure why she had prevented him from kissing her, not when she craved it with every inch of her being, but her instincts were certain.

Another kiss from Guy Partridge and she would be entirely under his spell.

"D-did your mother teach you how to talk to the ladies?" she asked.

"Not in the slightest," said Guy cheerfully. "No, it was my father. He was a charmer, I tell you—you think I am impressive—"

"No, I do not," Isabella interrupted. *There, a chance to cut him down to size.*

His eyes met hers, and her entire body quivered. "Don't lie to me, Isabella. I see the way you look at me. No, as I say, it was my father who knew the way to impress a woman, and as I had no siblings, I was taught everything he knew. After that, I had to learn the rest myself."

"No siblings?" repeated Isabella.

Goodness, she could hardly imagine such a thing. No siblings at all? Though she herself was the second-born, her sister Katarina had appeared so swiftly afterward that Isabella had no memory of fewer than two sisters.

They were always there, all three of them: always louder, more impressive, more daring. More beautiful.

"You have a sister, I think?"

Isabella laughed dryly. "I have three sisters, and eight cousins. All ladies."

Guy raised an eyebrow. "All ladies, you say?"

His words hit her hard. The sight of his eyes lighting up at the information of so many Fitzroy cousins—though, of course, all but two were married now, so they were technically not Fitzroys any longer—was intensely painful.

Of course he had no real interest in her, Isabella thought dully. Of course this was merely a means to gain access to the house, to other beautiful women. Someone like Guy would not care they were married; more, perhaps that gave him an additional thrill. There were men like that. She had read about them in the scandal sheets.

Isabella slumped against the window frame. Well, it had been pleasant while it lasted, the hope that Guy Partridge may actually care for her.

But it was over almost as soon as it had begun. He would never look at her while Caroline was in the place.

"Yes, all ladies," she said, attempting to keep bitterness from her voice. "All married, save two, though I believe one is engaged."

"And you," Guy pointed out. "My, my. How interesting."

A flicker of painful jealousy crept around Isabella's heart. All she wanted to do was keep him to herself, to have something of her own, a man of her own. Even if he never actually desired him, rather than the chase, he would be hers and hers alone.

"Yes, they are all coming here for Christmas," Isabella said. "You will be able to choose the best of the lot."

Guy grinned. "Good. I look forward to it."

How could he say such a thing? How could he look at her, risking her reputation by sitting here with him, nothing but a window frame between them in the dead of night—*her in her nightgown!*—and speak those words?

"Not that I need to wait," he continued, his voice low. "I have already found the best."

A dark, hungry, twisting desire roared in Isabella's heart, but she tried to push it aside. He did not mean that. It was just that flattery his father had taught him, as he had already admitted. Flattery designed for every lady, not special to her.

"Though I admit I am a little confused about something."

Isabella's eyes met his, and she tried to keep her voice level as she said, "Oh?"

"You," said Guy, pointing at her, keeping his finger just a few inches from her chest, which burned at the lack of his touch. "You are unmarried. Now that *does* surprise me."

She was not going to permit herself to be flattered.

"I suppose no one bothered to look at me in…in that way," she said.

Guy's gaze was fixed on hers. "Now that I find very hard to believe."

The moment became charged in a way Isabella did not understand. As though at any moment lightning would crackle from their hands, so close and yet so painfully apart.

"Isabella," Guy breathed.

She swallowed. She nodded, not trusting her voice.

"Will you let me in now?"

Oh, every part of her craved to let him in; not just into her bedchamber, but into her heart, her bed, her very body. Isabella knew just from that one kiss that Guy knew his way around a bed, around a woman's body.

She wanted to be touched by him, loved by him, to be taken to heights of pleasure she had not known existed by him.

But there was just enough common sense left in her to speak.

"No."

Guy sighed, hanging his head. "I thought you would say that."

A shy smile crept across Isabella's face. "So why did you ask?"

"Why, to hear you say it, of course," he said. "You may have said yes. I lost nothing with the asking."

Isabella nodded, hating that she had forbidden him. After all, he had been in her bedchamber before, had he not? What difference would it make if he was to do so again?

"Isabella, how quiet are you?" Guy asked suddenly.

It was such a strange question that Isabella could do naught but blink at first. "Quiet?"

He nodded.

Well, there was no harm in answering, was there? "Very quiet, I would—Guy!"

Isabella gasped his name, but quietly, understanding why he had asked such a question. It was impossible not to, now that he had reached out and lifted her nightgown skirt, moving his fingers swiftly along the thighs to that secret place right between her legs.

Guy groaned as Isabella stared, gasping for air. "God, you're wet, Isabella."

Shame, embarrassment, a hot sort of delicious agony rushed through her. She *was* wet—she could feel her own wetness as he gently stroked her curls, sliding one finger gently into her and making her whole body quiver.

Oh, this was too much! This was scandalous, this was disgraceful, this was...

"Oooh..." Isabella breathed, overtaken by the pleasure that rippled across her body.

Oh, this was far better than when she had touched herself. That had been timid, shy, almost unconscious, and with no real skill.

Guy had skill. His eyes were fixed on hers, drinking in her pleasure, every soft, quivering moan; his fingers teased the soft, wet folds of her lips, and Isabella shivered, clutching on to the sides of the windowsill.

"Guy, you mustn't—"

"I'll be the judge of what I mustn't, thank you," he said, desire dripping from every word. "And right now, you must not make a sound. Do you hear me, Isabella? Not a sound."

Isabella swallowed down the whimper she wanted to make and leaned back against the wall, struggling to keep her eyes open as she gently opened her legs, welcoming him in.

Welcomed in the pleasure that sparked every time his fingers danced across her—

"Guy!"

She could not help it. Two of his fingers, tight together, had entered her slick and willing special area, and a pulse of pleasure rocked her.

But his fingers had stilled. Gasping for breath, desperate for more, Isabella opened her eyes and looked at Guy.

There was a wicked grin on his face, but his eyes were serious. "Did I not tell you to be quiet?"

Isabella panted, heart fluttering, desperate for him to move again. Oh, she needed him to move again! She nodded, pursing her lips, then arched her back and whimpered as his fingers moved deeper inside her.

"Better," Guy breathed.

She did not know how she did it, but somehow Isabella managed to keep quiet as wave upon wave of pleasure rained down on her. It was too much, it was not enough, and Guy's fingers built a rhythm, slowly yet steadily, that increased in pace so gently she hardly noticed it at first.

And then she could do nothing but notice it, do nothing but feel the glory of his touch, the aching, twisting, sensual way her body responded, and it was growing, growing, and Isabella opened her mouth in an unspoken scream as ecstasy coursed through her body.

Her legs clenched around his hand, and she spasmed with the

pleasure, unable to hold it in.

Slowly, very slowly, Isabella opened her eyes and unclenched her legs.

Guy was still looking at her, eyes wide and full of lust, as he slowly drew his fingers from her. Without breaking his gaze, he slowly lifted his fingers to his mouth and licked them.

"As I said," came his hungry voice, "you taste wonderful."

CHAPTER FIVE

I SABELLA TOOK A deep breath and tried to reassure herself that this was precisely the sort of thing that a lady would do on a nice winter day. She was doing nothing radical—at least, nothing nearly so radical as the things she had done recently.

Witnessed an attack in the street.

Been teased by a stranger.

Been kissed by that stranger.

Been visited by that stranger, now no longer a stranger, in her bedchamber.

Permitted him to do such things to her last night…

"You must not make a sound. Do you hear me, Isabella? Not a sound."

Isabella lifted a hand to her chest as though that would some-how calm her heart rate. It did no such thing; but then, she had found it rather difficult to stay calm the last few days.

Ever since Guy Partridge entered her life, in truth.

It was remarkably difficult to do anything about the way that he looked at her, and moreover, the way her very soul responded to him when he did so.

"As I said, you taste wonderful."

That did not precisely mean it was logical, what she was doing. Ordering the carriage against her mother's wishes. Determining to go to Bath, without any of her family, without a chaperone, without anyone.

All because she could not stop thinking about a gentleman who had made her feel…

Isabella swallowed. "Everything."

She breathed the word in the carriage, alone, as though that made it less real—but there was nothing more real than Guy Partridge. Everything she knew of him, every moment she spent in his company, he was fast becoming more real than the rest of her life.

And so, yes, she had decided to spend the day in Bath. After all, what harm could it do? Christmas was coming, she told herself, and there were many reasons a lady may wish to go to Bath. Purchasing gifts. Visiting friends, or family. Going to the Pump Room.

Hunting down a gentleman who touched her in a way she had never believed…

The carriage rumbled into the town, over Pulteney Bridge and along Argyle Street. Isabella leaned over to the window, looking out at the crowds on the pavements. A small part of her believed, in truth, that she would see Guy immediately, walking along as though it was perfectly natural that they should meet.

If only they had agreed to such a thing, Isabella could not help but wishing. But after Guy pleasured her so utterly in the dead of night, she had been rather unable to think about such logical things, and he slipped away before she could say a word.

Though what precisely she would have said, Isabella could not tell…

"As I said, you taste wonderful."

Her cheeks burned as the carriage came to a halt. That he had said such a thing—done such a thing!

It was unheard of. Surely no other gentleman had ever done such a thing! Perhaps that was what made it all the more special, all the more daring.

And she wanted it again. Isabella had never done anything wild or rebellious in her life, but the mere hours they had been apart were agony, and she would not live without him.

"How long will you be, miss?"

Isabella smiled weakly as the driver opened the door, offering her a hand. Not until she had stepped out onto the pavement, blinking up into the unusually bright December day, did she speak.

"Oh, I don't know," she said as airily as she could manage. "I may well visit the Fitzroys, of course, so I am afraid you will have to wait here."

"I could always drop you off at—"

"No," Isabella cut in quickly. No, she did not need to see Uncle Rupert and Aunt Frances—nor endure their remarks about how little they saw her and how well she looked, for her age.

For her age. She had half expected her cousin Joy to intervene at that.

"No, thank you," Isabella added. "No, I would much rather stretch my legs a little. I shall not be more than a few hours, I believe."

Though what gave her that belief, she was not sure. She was being wild and rebellious, coming here to find Guy merely because she could not live a single day without him…

Which was ridiculous, Isabella tried to tell herself as the driver nodded and settled himself on top of the carriage. She could certainly live a day without Guy.

She just did not wish to.

But it was only now she had arrived at Bath, standing here on the pavement in the swirling crowd of people who clamored down the streets of the town, that she realized just how difficult it would be to find a man like him.

Why, beyond his name, Isabella knew nothing about him. Did not know where he had taken rooms, did not know his haunts, whether he was a member of any club.

Not that she could barge her way into a gentlemen's club!

But that did rather leave her at a loose end. Isabella meandered, her feet taking her to the Pump Room. She would have a look in the visitors book, see when he was last here.

Isabella did her best not to catch anyone's eye as they promenaded back and forth. She was unchaperoned, which was unusual, and the last thing she needed was for gossip about one of the Fitzroys to abound.

But it did not matter; she was not in the Pump Room for long. Although she wrote her name elegantly at the bottom of one page, even after turning back several, she could not see any name that she recognized.

Certainly no Guy Partridge.

Disappointment settling into her stomach, Isabella descended back to the street and took a deep breath.

It was very close to Christmas—just a few days. Really she should be with her family, not hunting around for a husband.

For Guy, Isabella amended swiftly, her cheeks warming. From the cold. Not because of a rather scandalous thought she had just had.

But after meandering around Sydney Gardens, Milsom Street, and the Assembly Rooms—there was a concert going on, not one she wished to interrupt—Isabella had to admit there was little point in remaining in town.

There was nowhere else she could think to look—and in a way, Isabella thought as she meandered back to the carriage, it was a relief.

After all, what could she have said to him if she *had* found him? That she had been looking for him? It was a very forward thing to do, and Guy would surely have had some witty quip to make about the whole thing.

"Ah, Miss Fitzroy," said her driver gratefully, rubbing his hands together.

A prickle of shame tightened around her heart. The poor man; she really should have thought about this more before she had set off. The man must be freezing!

"Did you enjoy your time in Bath?"

Isabella hesitated. "Yes. Yes, I suppose so, but I think it best I return home now."

Her driver nodded sagely. "Yes, I can smell it too."

She blinked. *Smell it?*

"The snow in the air," he said with a grin. "You have good instincts, Miss Fitzroy. You able to get in yourself?"

"Yes, thank you," said Isabella a little listlessly.

She had come all this way and for nothing—no Guy, no trace of him whatsoever. Perhaps she should have frequented the lanes to see whether anyone else was getting attacked, she thought darkly as she pulled open the carriage door and stepped in. That might have—

"You do indeed have good instincts, Miss Fitzroy," said Guy, lounging in the carriage with a lopsided grin on his face. "Very good."

Isabella almost slipped on the last step into the carriage. Only thanks to Guy's steadying hand, which he immediately reached out to balance her, was she prevented from falling.

"Steady as she goes," said Guy quietly, depositing her on the seat opposite him, before reaching past her to shut the door. "We wouldn't want you falling into my arms, would we?"

Isabella smiled weakly and stared, unable to believe what she was seeing.

Guy Partridge…in her carriage! Waiting for her!

Every part of her body was tingling as the memory of what his fingers had been able to do to her rushed through her mind.

"It has been some time since I was gifted with the pleasure of your mouth. Here, let me taste again."

Guy's eyes glittered. "Thinking of a certain moment, are we?"

Isabella swallowed and attempted to draw herself up. This was her carriage, she was a Fitzroy, and she was not going to be cowed within it. There was a boldness in her, somewhere, inherited from her mother—and a prestige from her father.

She was not going to be overwhelmed.

"You…you know you cannot be here, Guy," she said softly.

Before Guy could reply, her driver said, "What was that, Miss

Fitzroy?"

Guy glanced at the front of the carriage, then back to Isabella. She could have him removed, she knew. Just a simple word to her driver and Guy would be thrown out—and told never to darken her doorway again.

Isabella smiled. But that was not what she wanted.

"I take it you also are travelling to Chalcroft?" she asked loftily, tapping the roof of the carriage.

It jerked forward, the rumbling of the wheels and the clattering of the horses' hooves making it impossible now for her driver to hear her. To hear them.

Guy looked remarkably impressed. "I thought you said I cannot be in here."

"Oh, you cannot, it is most irregular," said Isabella with a nervous smile. Was this flirting, then? She had never done it before, never managed to find a gentleman who wished to engage in such a thing.

But Guy…

"Oh, so there is the same rule for your carriage as there is your bedchamber?" Guy raised an eyebrow. "Well, I had a rather wonderful time not being in your bedchamber last night. I wonder whether that is something we could repeat."

Heat rushed through Isabella's body; her pulse quickened and her rather disobligingly traitorous heart leapt.

To repeat last night here, in the carriage…well, no one was going to discover them, were they?

Her resolve hardened. She may be delighted to see him—far too delighted, in truth—but that did not mean Guy could have his own way.

"You cannot come to Chalcroft," she said.

"And why not?" Guy said with a grin. "'Tis nothing wrong with wishing to visit the charming little church there. I will have you know, I am a great admirer of ecclesiastical architecture."

Isabella smiled; she could not help herself. He really was the most disobliging, irritating, wonderful man she had ever met.

And he had kissed her. Touched her, brought her to ecstasy.

How would she ever live without him?

"Well, I wish you well on your exploration of arches and naves," she said, hardly able to believe she was able to speak so calmly.

He had hidden in her carriage!

"Thank you," said Guy, bowing his head.

"Just do not expect to be introduced to my sisters or my parents while you are in the area," said Isabella, hoping her smile showed her words to be the flirtation she intended. "Or else they will start to have…expectations."

A quiver of something rather akin to expectations of her own rippled through her. What was she doing, having a clandestine meeting with a gentleman in a carriage?

But was it any less outrageous than a clandestine meeting with a gentleman in her bedchamber? Isabella could hardly tell, but as the streets of Bath disappeared from the window and fields started to appear, it was easy to believe that they were the only people in the world.

Just the two of them. Guy and her.

Guy raised an eyebrow. "Expectations, you say?"

There was a teasing tone to his voice. Isabella held his gaze as she repeated, "Yes, expectations."

"And do you want them to?"

His question was swift, immediate, and Isabella was hardly sure how to answer such a thing. If she replied in the affirmative, it would reveal she had much deeper feelings for this man before her than she wished him to know. She would only be disappointed, after all.

But if she replied in the negative, would he think her heartless—uninterested?

"Of course not," she said airily, but smiling as mischievously as she could manage. "That would be outrageous."

"Oh, right, good," Guy said easily. "As long as we are all on the same page. You do not wish me to be introduced to your parents, you have no expectations of me, and I...I can't stop myself, Isabella."

She did not need to ask what Guy could not stop himself from doing; it was obvious the moment his lips touched hers.

Guy had moved to sit beside her, was cupping her cheeks, and his mouth ravaged hers, giving such pleasure that Isabella had no choice but to moan. His tongue, eager and scalding hot, demanded entrance, and she gave in to him, welcoming him, giddy with the proximity of his body, his scent, knowing this was not something well-behaved ladies did.

But she did not wish to be well behaved any more.

The kiss lasted far longer than Isabella could have imagined, and when it finally broke, her breathing was shallow and rapid.

"Guy," she murmured.

His eyes were blazing, eager, hungry for something she was not certain she could give him. "Isabella."

What was she supposed to do with him—with all these feelings surging in her chest, pulsing in her body, throbbing between her legs?

It was impossible to speak what she wanted, to ask for something certain and secure—a proposal of marriage, for example.

But more than that, Isabella wanted him to kiss her again, yet knew he should not. He should not! Gentlemen should not go around just kissing ladies!

The carriage rumbled over a stone, jolting slightly to the left, and Isabella smiled weakly up at the man who was fast becoming her sole reason for waking up in the morning. "We mustn't."

"We must," pointed out Guy, as though it were a well-reasoned argument.

"No, we—Guy, we mustn't." Isabella gasped as he dipped his head to kiss her neck, to nuzzle her skin, to taste her once again. "Guy...we mustn't..."

It did not seem to matter. There was no real heart in her words, after all, no real desire for this to end. Quite to the contrary, Isabella yearned for this to continue forever, for them to never reach their destination.

It was a short hour back to Chalcroft indeed, if this was how she could spend it…

"Isabella," groaned Guy, his hands tight around her waist.

For some reason, hearing her name like that brought her to her senses. No, they really should not, could not do such a thing.

"Guy—Guy," she said firmly.

Guy lifted his head, eyes desperate for more, and smiled at her. "Isabella."

Isabella's stomach lurched, but she tried to push aside the sensation. "You cannot kiss m-me on the neck."

A wicked smile spread across Guy's face. "That is not a problem."

He leaned forward and captured her lips with his, and Isabella indulged for a moment in the heady sensations before pushing him away.

"You know what I mean! You cannot kiss me on the mouth either."

Something odd flickered across Guy's face. Though Isabella could barely think, enclosed as she was in Guy's arms, the memory of his kiss still burned on her lips, she thought she saw a knowing smile on his face.

"I understand. I won't kiss you on the mouth."

Isabella relaxed as Guy released his hands from her waist and moved off the seat beside her—but gasped as he then did something most unaccountable.

He knelt down in the carriage footwell.

"Guy, what are you—Guy!"

Isabella clutched at the seat in shock as Guy lifted her skirts and ducked underneath.

"You said not to kiss you on the mouth," came Guy's voice from beneath her gown, as he gently kissed her knee.

Isabella swallowed, unable to think, unable to move, desperate to continue but knowing he absolutely should not—

"And so I'm not," said Guy quietly, gently parting her knees.

"Guy," breathed Isabella, hardly able to speak as his lips caressed her thighs, moving slowly up her body, closer and closer to—"Guy!"

Her back arched and her whole body quivered with anticipation as his lips met her curls. Oh, God, she already knew what she was about to experience, at least a small part of it, and Isabella cried out in exquisite pleasure as his tongue entered her.

This was too much, and yet not enough. As the carriage continued to rattle along the country lanes toward Chalcroft, Isabella twisted her hips to welcome Guy's tongue deeper into her secret place.

Where only last night his fingers had made short work of fiddling her to pleasure, Isabella moaned as Guy's tongue did just the same, though it was deeper somehow, more decadent, more intimate.

"As I said, you taste wonderful."

He could certainly taste her now, and Isabella could hear him, feel him moaning as he tasted more of her wet glory.

"Guy…"

Isabella could not help it; her body craved him and there was not much she could do to dam the pleasure pressuring her body.

"Guy!"

For the second time in her life, Isabella threw back her head and welcomed the waves of agonizing pleasure overtaking her. This time her sight disappeared, just for a moment; white spots appeared in her vision and gently faded as Guy's tongue ceased its movements.

The carriage was filled with no noise, save Isabella's jagged panting.

Guy emerged from her skirts. "Damn."

"Damn?" Isabella managed.

His eyes darkened. "I want to do that again."

"Wh—Again?"

He was mad; there was no possibility of her feeling that again, Isabella was certain, as her very ribs ached at the sudden pleasure that had rocked her. No, she would need hours, perhaps days to recover from—

"Guy," Isabella moaned.

His tongue was inside her once again, slower this time, but no less sensual. Precisely where it should be.

CHAPTER SIX

"—AND ABOUT TIME, too. I was starting to worry!"

Isabella smiled weakly as her mother rose from the armchair. "I told you, Mama, the roads can be a little icy, but there was no reason to think—"

"Olivia's children are fine, very fine indeed, but it is time for their mother to come back for them! You wait until you have daughters, my girl," said Leonora as she strode across the drawing room. "Then you may lecture me on worrying about your children."

Her mother disappeared into the hall just in time to miss Isabella's pained face.

She was not going to let it upset her, though her hands shook as she rose to her feet and smoothed down her gown. She was not going to be upset. She was not going to take it to heart. Her mother simply did not understand how painful those words were.

Even now, when she was having a dalliance with a gentleman completely unbeknownst to her family, matrimony was never far from her mind…

Isabella swallowed. The light had faded swiftly this evening, but it had not dulled the memory of that morning. Of what she had shared with Guy in the carriage.

A carriage she would now never be able to sit in without thinking of him, the way he kissed her, the pleasure he drew from her body…

It was the fire, Isabella thought with a wry smile. That was what she could blame her scalding cheeks on. The fire. Certainly not the memory of being exquisitely pleasured not once, but thrice between here and Bath.

Why, she had not even realized how swiftly her body could recover from such—

"There she is—you did not wish to welcome us, then?"

Isabella looked up at her eldest sister, Olivia, round with child and with two little ones holding each of her hands.

"My, you look flushed," said Olivia conversationally.

"Fire," said Isabella hurriedly. If only she had control of her tongue, she could have spoken that far more reasonably.

If only she had Guy's technique with a tongue…

"Yes, I suppose the fire is a little warm," said Olivia, depositing her children on the sofa and embracing her sister. "Are the others here yet?"

Isabella shook her head. The entirety of Chalcroft had spent the afternoon waiting, eagerly, for any sign of the three Fitzroy sisters who had married and left their childhood home, and their mother was still standing in the hall, hoping for another one of her brood to return.

"I told you we would be early," said Luke with a laugh.

Isabella grinned at her brother-in-law. "Not that you would know it from the way Mama carries on."

"I do not carry on! Me, carry on?" Leonora had returned, a grandchild in her arms. "I do not believe I have ever carried on in my entire—"

"Was that another carriage?" said Isabella swiftly.

Her mother broke into a smile. "Was it?"

She disappeared back into the hall, and Isabella sagged with relief. Soon all three of her sisters would be here, ready to take the pressure of their parents' focus from her.

"Did you actually hear a carriage?" asked Olivia, raising an eyebrow.

"No," admitted Isabella with a laugh before kissing her two nieces on their foreheads. "But Kitty is due here any moment, and unless—There's one!"

The hallway erupted with noise just a few minutes later.

"Oh, and the roads, Mama, utterly dreadful! I told Isaac, I said to him, if it was not Christmas at Chalcroft I would say turn around this minute, because—Olivia's here, then?"

Isabella smiled a little wearily. Olivia, her husband, and their four children; Katarina, or Kitty when she was in a good mood, her husband and their little boy and twins; and Maria, her husband—the least favorite of Isabella's brothers-in-law—and their two sons.

The Fitzroy family would be whole again, and further increased on Christmas Eve, when the London and Bath branches of the family would be coming for a week.

Noise, and laughter, and delight, and children rushing about all over the place. Isabella would end up playing the role of nursemaid to a few of them and confidante to a few others, her parents would laugh gleefully at absolutely anything a child did, and she would be regaled with stories of husbands and children until she could take no more.

"And there's Maria!"

Olivia's exclamation brought Isabella out of her thoughts, and she stepped to the window beside her sister. "I did not expect her so soon."

"I suppose it is a long way," said Olivia with a smile. "Not so for us, of course. Why, our estate is only—"

"Kitty is closest," pointed out her husband as a daughter demanded his attention.

Olivia frowned slightly. "Yes, but theirs has no west wing, not like ours."

Isabella's smile became a little more forced. That was always the problem with Olivia: she was always so interested in being right, proper, the best in Society and the best *of* Society.

She had only become more irritating when she became a

lady.

But then, she was Isabella's sister—they all were. Isabella could not help but smile as Maria entered the room, her sons trailing behind her looking a little nervous of all the chatter in the drawing room, but swiftly being pulled into a game of tag with their cousins.

"Ah, we're all here, then?"

All Isabella's sisters cried out with delight as their father appeared, rushing at him and pulling him into their arms, and she laughed to watch them.

There was something about everyone coming home, the entire Fitzroy family in just a few days. Isabella knew they had no titles, no fabulous wealth, but something tied them together that was far more powerful than that.

Affection.

In a startling moment she could not have predicted, Isabella's imagination attempted to place Guy Partridge in such a scene. Would he get on with her brothers-in-law? Would her sisters like him? Would he play with the children, rushing around like a tiger as they squealed with delight... Would he speak to her father about politics, her mother about the garden?

A strange sort of twist clenched Isabella's stomach. It was hard to imagine. The Guy she knew, the man who visited her bedchamber, who kissed her in such exquisite ways, did not appear to belong to the real world.

She could no easier imagine him as part of the Fitzroy family than the regent.

But if matrimony was not something she could seriously consider, what on earth was she doing?

"Goodness, you look strange, Issy," commented Kitty as she pulled her into a rough hug. "What's on your mind?"

Isabella smiled weakly. She had never considered asking her sisters for advice before; in truth, she had never needed to. There were no gentlemen attempting to break the door down to get to her, after all.

But she certainly could not speak to either of her parents about Guy, and if she did not ask someone soon what this all meant, what on earth she was supposed to do about it, then she was certain she would scream.

And the last thing she needed was for her whole family to think she was wild...

"Mama," said Isabella.

Leonora looked up from tickling one of her grandsons. "Yes?"

"I do believe Isaac is the perfect person to advise you on extending the stables," said Isabella.

How the thought had entered her mind, she had no idea— but it was clear there was no possibility of speaking anything like what was on her mind with her brothers-in-law here.

Especially not Walter. She liked him, as much as she could, but Isabella would never forget how he had been a part of having gossip about her printed in the papers. No matter how many times Maria said that he was sorry.

No, if she was going to ask her sisters' advice—though how she would frame it, she still had not decided—she needed all the men out of the room.

"Oh, I would have thought Luke would be far better," said Olivia immediately, her natural competitiveness surfacing. "No offence, of course, Isaac."

"None taken," said Isaac affably. "But I would imagine Walter just as able to—"

"Wonderful," said Isabella swiftly. "You can all go—Mama, what a wonderful chance to get the advice of all three of your sons."

It took a gentle amount of chivvying to get them out of the drawing room, and just as the door closed on Walter, Maria glanced at Isabella with a far-too-knowing look.

Isabella flushed. Maria was the quietest of the four sisters, the most observant. The sister most likely to point out something you would much rather she did not.

"Maria, do you...do you not think Papa should take the children to the morning room where they are less likely to knock something precious over?" Isabella asked.

There was a moment—just a moment—of understanding between them.

Maria nodded. "I quite agree. Come on, Papa, lead out your mice like the Pied Piper!"

It appeared their father did not need much encouragement. His many grandchildren giggled away, trotting out in a line, one by one, and Isabella closed the door to the hall with a sigh of relief.

Quiet descended on the drawing room, devoid as it now was of parents, brothers-in-law, and numerous grandchildren.

Kitty sighed as she fell onto the sofa. "What a marvelous idea of yours, Isabella."

Isabella blinked. How on earth had her sister realized what she had been planning?

"I must say, it is a capital one," said Olivia, lowering herself in a ladylike way into an armchair, then sagging against it. "Just a few minutes without children to care for—"

"And the husbands," cut in Maria with a shy smile.

"Oh, the husbands are sometimes the worst," said Kitty with a giggle. "Worth at least three children when it comes to chaos!"

Isabella smiled weakly as her three sisters laughed. It was all very well, their laughing about the difficulties of having a husband, but it was rather awkward. After all, it was not as though she had such problems to share.

"Oh, I am sorry, Issy," said Olivia, her smile gone. "We did not mean to—"

"Please, think nothing of it," said Isabella, trying to smile as naturally as she could.

Her three sisters were all seated together by the fire, and she joined them, desperately trying to think about how to begin the conversation she wished to have.

Certainly not directly. She could hardly admit that she was being courted by—But no, Guy was not courting her, was he?

Seducing her. Making love to her. Making her feel…

Isabella's cheeks warmed. Such things that she would never speak of in public!

"I can imagine just how difficult they can be," she said delicately. "Yet, I suppose, you knew of their foibles before you married them. Did you not?"

"Livvy did," pointed out Kitty. "How long have we known Luke—ten years?"

"Oh, at least," Olivia said with a smile. "And yet in all that time—"

"But you, Kitty, and Maria, you met your husbands and swiftly agreed to marry them," interrupted Isabella. They did not need to suffer through another monologue on how wonderful Luke was. They had heard it all before. "You decided quickly, I think, they were right for you."

Kitty grinned. "Well, I am not sure I had much choice, you know. After all, I had been bedded by the man."

"Kitty!"

"Oh, don't you Kitty me," she said good-naturedly as Olivia looked aghast. "I have children now. Do you not think I have done it yet?"

Olivia flushed slightly and glanced at Isabella. "But Issy…she has not—"

"I did not kiss a man until Walter," said Maria quietly. All eyes turned to her, and she pinked slightly, but continued, "And he bedded me before we were married."

"Maria!" Isabella exclaimed.

She could hardly believe it of her sister. Maria, the quiet one, the gentle one, the one the entire family had never believed would marry! Bedded by Walter…before they were wed?

Slowly, the three sisters turned to look at Olivia, who flushed darkly.

"Oh, fine," she said, not looking at any of them. "Luke and I… Well, it was obvious we would marry; there was no possibility of—"

"So all three of you lost your innocence before you were married?" Isabella asked.

It was impossible to believe; if she had not heard it from each of their own mouths, she would never have credited it.

But she could not deny the truth. Despite all appearing to be paragons of virtue, despite never having given any hint of what had occurred—save for Kitty—all three of her sisters had permitted themselves the pleasures of the flesh before they walked up an aisle.

In a strange way, it made Isabella feel a little better. After all, it appeared she was not quite the radical, rebellious daughter she had believed herself to be.

"But why do you ask such questions, Issy?"

Isabella started. Olivia was looking at her most severely, and there was a look on Kitty's face she did not like.

"Ask?" Isabella repeated, buying time. "I did not ask—"

"You brought up the subject of husbands," Kitty said with a wry smile. "My goodness, Isabella, is there something you want to tell us?"

"No," Isabella said swiftly. "I just… I met someone. A gentleman."

All three of her sisters squealed.

"A gentleman!" crowed Kitty.

"I never thought I would see the day," said Olivia—rather unkindly, to Isabella's mind.

"Tell us all about him," said Maria eagerly. "Is he a gentleman? Or is he in trade?"

"Is he handsome and tall?" Olivia said with a laugh. "That's very important, trust me."

"Isabella is far less shallow than you, Liv. She will care more about his heart than his manhood!"

"Kitty!"

Isabella flushed at the onslaught. She had known it would be a risk speaking to her sisters about Guy Partridge—and she certainly would not be revealing his name—but it was pleasant, in a way, to share this with them.

Something she had never thought she would share.

"Ignore them and tell me the things that matter," said Maria, leaning forward.

Isabella swallowed. *The things that mattered.* How could she decide what mattered? In truth, she did not know very much that she could reveal in the first place.

Struck suddenly by the realization that she essentially knew five things about him—his name, his charity to the poor, that he fought remarkably well, his sad family story, and how he kissed like the devil—Isabella hesitated.

She was swiftly falling in love with him, she knew, yet how could she find such affection for a man she barely knew?

Oh, love at first sight happened, occasionally, Isabella was sure, but that was not the case here. Was it?

"Has he offered you anything in the way of affection?"

"Kitty Emmett!"

"I meant assurances, Olivia. Do not spark up at me," said Kitty with a sarcastic smile. "You knew what I meant, I am sure, Issy. Has he spoken of love, affection? Matrimony?"

Isabella hesitated. He had spoken of his desire for her, how well she tasted, but that was all. No words of promise or commitment had passed Guy's lips.

Was that something that should halt her eager heart?

"No," she said softly, and hated to see the visible disappointment in her sisters' eyes. "No, he has not."

CHAPTER SEVEN

THE LOUDEST YAWN Isabella had ever heard echoed around the drawing room.

"Goodness, who let off the cannon?" said Kitty sleepily.

Isabella smiled, curled up in the armchair nearest the fire. It was always her seat, had been for years, when she had been forced to fight her sisters for it. Now they had all gained husbands and left Chalcroft, it had become her seat—and most surprisingly, her sisters no longer fought her for it when they returned.

Maria scowled waspishly. "My yawn was not that loud."

"I think your neighbors in Wells can still hear it." Kitty grinned, a sleeping child in her lap.

Isabella glanced quickly at Maria to see whether the conversation would descend into an argument, but it appeared her youngest sister was far too tired for such nonsense.

It was, after all, very late. The dinner her parents had put on for the ten of them—the children dined in the breakfast room, to great hilarity, according to Cook—had been sumptuous, large, and with a great deal of wine.

Now they were seated lazily around the drawing room, a few children in laps or on sofas—those who had been permitted to stay up because of colds, or toothache, or whatever excuse her nieces and nephews could concoct.

Isabella smiled. They were definitely Fitzroys, even if they held different names.

But, as was always the way when she and her sisters got to-gether, there was very little incentive for anyone to go upstairs. The fear of missing out on a conversation, a snippet of gossip, kept them all here. But she was wise enough to know that as soon as one person gave in—

"Right, that's it," said Kitty loudly, rising to her feet as Maria gave another huge yawn. "I cannot stay down here a moment listening to Maria yawn."

"I barely yawned at all that time!" protested Maria, though there was a sheepish grin on her face. "Did I, Issy?"

Isabella smiled. "I'm near yawning myself just hearing yours."

Gentle chuckles murmured around the room as Walter rose and offered his wife his arm. "Come on, m'dear. Let's leave these people to their midnight vigil."

"Oh no, I'm going," Kitty said. "Maria can yawn all she likes down here!"

"You don't both have to go," pointed out Isaac, grinning at his wife. "As long as one of you—"

"What do you think, Issy?"

Isabella smiled gently at Kitty's forceful question. She knew far better than to get involved in one of Kitty's debates, especially when her sister was this tired. She had more than enough evidence throughout her life that it would not end well.

"I think we should all go to bed," said Isabella.

"Capital idea," said their mother, rising and stretching out with a yawn. "Goodness, I do struggle to keep up with you young ones."

"Olivia's being very quiet about the whole thing," their father remarked. "Where is…"

Everyone's eyes turned to Olivia. She was fast asleep, her mouth slightly open.

Isabella laughed with everyone, and for a moment, it was as though everything was right with the world. No matter their faults, she did love her family: parents, sisters, nieces and nephews. Even her brothers-in-law were mostly palatable. Her cousins were wonderful; they had made wonderful matches. And they'd all be here soon. It wouldn't be long before Chalcroft was packed to the rafters. But then—

"Right, every husband grab a wife, preferably his own, and head upstairs," announced Kitty with a laugh. "That way everyone will… Oh."

Isabella ensured a smile was on her face as everyone looked at her. "It's fine."

Kitty's face was racked with guilt. "Issy, I did not—"

"I know," Isabella said, her false smile remaining. "Go on. Bedtime."

There was a certain amount of kerfuffle, quiet conversation, leave taking and well wishing, gathering up of children and hunting down lost fans, but Isabella remained seated by the fire. She had no need to get involved, as had been made positively clear.

"Right, every husband grab a wife, preferably his own, and head upstairs…"

Her sister had meant nothing by it, Isabella knew, but that did not prevent it stinging.

She was well aware she was the odd one out. Her lack of husband put her off-kilter with the rest of them, and it was never more obvious than in moments like this.

"Go on with you," her father was saying, shooing the last grandchild. "Go on."

Isabella's gaze drifted to the dying fire as both their parents returned to the sofa opposite her. Which was most odd, now she came to think about it. Was it not her mother who had said that she was tired of staying up with them all?

"Isabella," said Leonora.

Isabella looked up to see a serious look on her mother's face, and braced herself for another one of her parents' "talks."

They used to be rare. Every year or so, her parents would sit her down and try to encourage her to do something to find a husband. *Go out to town—with a chaperone, of course—accept one of your sisters' invitations to stay, go to Town to visit one of the London Fitzroys…*

In short, do anything but stay here at Chalcroft, getting older and older…

Isabella forced a smile back on her face. Then the "talks" had become more frequent. Every six months. Every month. Then, since the beginning of this year, she had not received any such talk. She had been pleased at first, until the thought crossed her mind that her parents had given up.

But no, it appeared she was going to have another one of those talks. Much good may it do her.

"Isabella," said William with a wry smile.

"Mama and Papa," said Isabella with just as much seriousness. "May I help you?"

Her parents exchanged a look, and her heart sank. Was it that bad? Were they tired of her, the shame of having her here, a spinster?

"We wanted to ensure…well, that you were quite well."

Isabella blinked at her mother's words. *Quite well?* What did that mean? What were they concerned about—that she had a fever but had been managing to hide it?

"Quite well," she repeated.

Her father nodded. "We know how much you enjoy having the family here, but comments like Kitty's…they will only become more frequent when the whole family is here."

"Not from unkindness," cut in her mother, eyes desperate. "By accident, but still…"

Isabella swallowed. They were worried she was going to become offended by the sheer number of married people at Chalcroft this Christmas.

Well, perhaps they should be having that conversation with her cousin Joy, she thought a little uncharitably. She was the one who was sparking irritability whenever anyone mentioned it. Isabella, so far, had managed to keep her tongue to herself.

"Please do not concern yourself about a thing," Isabella said placidly, as though it made no difference to her if her family teased her or not. As though the barbs never entered her heart. "I am quite happy to have everyone here, and in truth, I welcome such comments."

William blinked at his daughter. "You do?"

"I do," said Isabella, crossing her fingers under her hand in her lap. "I like people to say what they think and feel; you know that. There should not be any topic the entire family is avoiding just for me and Sophia, though I think Aunt Selina's letter said—"

"And your cousin Joy."

"And my cousin Joy." She nodded. "So there you are. You can see that I will not be alone in my…situation."

It was kind of them, Isabella tried to remind herself. They cared for her so much, worried about her, hoped everything would change for her. But there would be no husband waiting for her at the end of this Christmas season…unless Guy…

Heat seared her cheeks, but she tried to keep her breathing calm, despite the great provocation. Was it wrong, to hope Guy would be making a visit to her bedchamber that evening? That he perhaps was already in the pear tree, waiting for her?

Oh, the thought of enduring an evening without him was agony. The idea of missing his kisses, the need to be together…it was more than she could ever have dreamt of.

"Well. Right. Good," said William a little uncertainly.

Isabella watched him exchange a glance with her mother, then the two of them leaned back into the sofa, obviously relieved.

"In that case, I'll go up," said Leonora wearily. "I really am most tired, and there is so much to do tomorrow! The—"

"Wreath making," chorused her husband and daughter.

Leonora's eyes sparkled. "Do not even try to pretend you do not enjoy it, for I will not believe you. Goodnight, Isabella."

"Goodnight, Mama," said Isabella with a smile.

The door closed behind her, and William sighed. "It is good

of you to say all that. For your mother's sake."

Isabella's smile became a little weary. Honestly, what did she have to do to be believed? "I spoke the truth, Papa."

"Of course you did," said her father, waving a hand as though that ended the conversation. "By the by, my dear, I wanted to let you know that after Christmas and the New Year, I want you to move to a different bedchamber for a few days."

A different bedchamber? It was most strange. Oh, Isabella sometimes moved along that corridor to air out a bedchamber, or if she had a headache—the light was so very different down that side of the house—but it was rarely arranged in advance.

"Of course, Papa, but why?"

"I am going to have some men in that room," said William. "It's high time I organized it, in truth."

"Men?"

"To cut down the pear tree."

"No!"

Isabella had not meant to speak so loudly, had not intended to rise to her feet in indignation, heart pounding, fists clenched.

But she had, and her father stared in complete surprise. "Isabella?"

"Why would you want to cut down such a beautiful tree?" she said, words spilling out as her lungs tightened.

Cut down the pear tree? Remove not only a beautiful tree that often—well, occasionally—gave fruit, but remove the way for Guy Partridge to reach her?

No, it was outrageous. The very idea of removing her link to such a man was abhorrent; she would not allow it. Just a few more days and then it would be over, the pear tree gone, and Guy unable to reach her bedchamber? No.

"I did not realize you were so attached to that old thing," said William. "You have never mentioned it before."

Isabella swallowed. How could she explain this to her father without saying anything about Guy? The absolute last thing she wanted to reveal was that she was being thoroughly pleasured each and every time her lover—for what else could she call Guy?—visited.

"I…I…" Isabella cleared her throat and desperately hoped her wits would rescue her, but it was so late, she could hardly think. "I love that pear tree."

"But is it not preventing sunshine from reaching your bedchamber?" asked her father. "I would have thought in the summer your bedchamber must be cold—"

"Wonderfully cold," interrupted Isabella desperately. "Not too hot, as so many other bedchambers are, and for my headaches—"

"Let's talk about this in the morning," said her father, rising to his feet. "We're both tired. Come on."

Isabella had no option but to follow her father out of the drawing room and up the wide, sweeping staircase. He kissed her forehead before turning left toward his bedchamber, and Isabella listlessly walked down the corridor in the opposite direction, to her own.

She did not bother getting into her nightgown. She made straight for the window casing, lifting up the sash and letting in the freezing December night air. It would be Christmas Eve tomorrow; the last of the Fitzroys would be arriving at Chalcroft, and then it would be New Year…

And then this sensual adventure she was on would come to an end.

Five minutes later, a gentleman started clambering up the pear tree.

"Guy," whispered Isabella.

He grinned as he reached the window and stole a hasty, heated kiss. "You called?"

But Isabella was not in the mood for jesting. She had to grab hold of him, take everything she could while he was still here.

While he could still reach her.

Sitting on the casement as Guy settled himself on the sill, Isabella leaned forward, all hesitancy forgotten. She kissed him hard on the mouth. Guy was forced to reach out and grab a branch and the sill in an effort to keep himself steady, but she did not care. All Isabella wanted was to take as much pleasure as possible.

When the kiss broke, her breath was short and his eyes bright.

"My word, I had not expected that," he managed to say.

The words came spilling out before she could stop them. "This might be one of the last times you can visit."

Guy's smile faltered. "I beg your pardon?"

"My father, he—"

"He does not know about us?"

Isabella smiled to hear the panic in Guy's voice, to luxuriate in the way he said "us." There was an *us*. Precisely what form that would be, she did not know…but it was a start.

"No, he has no idea—none of my family have any suspicion," she said. "They cannot see the difference in me, the change…"

Her voice trailed away as she caught herself revealing far more than she had intended.

After all, she could barely put her finger on the difference, let alone explain it to him. There was something about her now, now she had experienced such pleasure, such intimacy.

Something about the way she looked at the world, perhaps. It was not with the same innocence she had held before. The whole world seemed brighter, bolder, lighter. Whenever she was with Guy, Isabella felt…desired. Passionate. Eager for the next day.

"He is going to have the pear tree cut down."

A life of trudging from one dull dinner party to the next had somehow become something far more interesting, and that was all because of him. Guy Partridge. The man who had clambered up her pear tree and taken—and given—more pleasure than Isabella had even known existed.

"He wants to cut the pear tree down?"

Isabella forced herself back into the moment. Guy was looking at her with genuine confusion, and was that…pain? How much did she mean to him?

"My father thinks it is blocking out the light," she said softly.

Guy rolled his eyes. "What an irritatingly reasonable excuse."

In any other circumstance, Isabella would have laughed—but she could not laugh at this. A dull pain had settled in her stomach the moment her father started talking about removing the pear tree—a fear that her life, which only now seemed to be beginning, was about to come to an abrupt end.

"He says he will have it cut down after the New Year," said Isabella in a low voice. "And my family—my cousins, aunts, uncles—they are all arriving tomorrow. Christmas Eve."

"So that gives us tonight," said Guy, his eyes fixed on hers.

Isabella swallowed. "Yes."

Tonight. After tonight, whatever this was—and she was still not sure—would be over.

"I will not allow that to happen."

Isabella snapped her gaze up from her lap to Guy's face, which was set in a determined expression. "You won't?"

Guy shook his head. He reached out to cup her cheek, and his voice shook as he said, "You think I will allow this pear tree to be cut down—my route to you? Isabella, you have no idea how I…how much I…"

Isabella sat as still as she could, barely breathing, as she watched Guy struggle for words. Was this it? Was he about to reveal to her that he was starting to care for her…that he could perhaps one day—

"I love you, Isabella," Guy said.

Isabella's jaw fell open. "No you don't."

The words slipped out of her mouth so quickly, Guy laughed. "You don't think so?"

"But, I mean—Well, we only met a week ago! Less than that!" protested Isabella, hardly knowing why she was arguing with a gentleman who wished to profess his love to her. "You can't fall in love with someone in just three or four days!"

Her heart was pounding as she spoke, rebelling against her

words most furiously. Why could he not? Were not such matches made all the time? Was it not possible that fate, or chance, something stronger, had been drawing them together all this while, and finally found them in that lane in Bath?

"What do you mean, you cannot fall in love with someone that quickly?" said Guy, his mouth in a lopsided grin and his eyes blazing. "I have. Haven't you?"

CHAPTER EIGHT

GUY'S WORDS ECHOED in Isabella's mind, unable to be ignored.

"What do you mean, you cannot fall in love with someone that quickly? I have. Haven't you?"

She stared at him illuminated by the wintry moonlight, and tried to take in what he had said, but it was impossible. People did not fall in love that quickly! It was simply madness.

He could not be speaking the truth.

But there was no lie in his eyes. Isabella looked carefully at them, bright in the moonlight, and saw nothing but honesty and truth. A little discomfort, true, and a heap of desire, but that was how Guy always looked at her.

Heat seared Isabella's cheeks. That *was* how he always looked at her, right from the very first moment she had ever clapped eyes on him.

What was it he had said to her, the very first time they met?

"I am sorry you had to witness that, miss. Not a pleasant sight."

"I wouldn't say that."

And since that moment, she had been transfixed. Well, perhaps it was the kiss that had done that, Isabella thought wryly. But with every succeeding day, she was brought more and more into his power, and now he was saying such wonderful things…

"What do you mean, you cannot fall in love with someone that

quickly? I have. Haven't you?"

Isabella swallowed. She was not going to let this go to her head. "That only happens in stories."

"And where do the stories come from?" Guy said urgently, as though his life depended on it. "Isabella, do you think I expected this to happen? Do you think I knew in that Bath lane I would find someone who—who utterly captured my heart?"

Those words, glorious to hear, echoed in her mind, but Isabella knew she could give them no credence. A man who kissed like that, who touched like that, had surely said those same words to others before.

And it was that thought which doused her hopes and dreams with cold water.

"Have you ever been in love before?"

Isabella knew his response before he gave it, saw the hesitation in his eyes, the way he glanced away from her before returning to look at her face.

"I thought it, before," Guy said quietly. "But I never felt it. I never spoke it, never bared my soul to someone as I am to you."

It was flattering; it was delightful; it was hard not to wish it was true. Isabella's mind whirled with half-formed thoughts, and she desperately attempted to untangle them, knowing she could barely conceive of what to say, let alone what her heart was feeling.

"You feel it too, I know you do," said Guy, dropping his hand from her cheek and taking one of her hands in his. "I know you feel affection for me, Isabella—"

"Just because I feel…feel warm when you touch me, and desire when you…" Isabella said hotly, not certain how to finish such a sentence. "That does not mean—"

"You're right, it's more than that," said Guy earnestly, eyes wide. "Tell me. How did you feel when your father said he was going to cut down the pear tree?"

Isabella swallowed. "As…as though the world was ending."

The words had slipped from her mouth, so visceral was her

reaction. She could not describe the fear, the anger at her father for considering such a thing.

To tear her away from Guy—it could not be borne.

A smile was slowly creeping across Guy's face. "And I felt the same way when you told me of his decision. Do you not see, Isabella? What is love but a desperate need to be with that person? The knowledge that without them life is not worth living, food loses all taste, flowers lose their bloom, literature loses its spark!"

Isabella stared, transfixed, at the man before her. These were heady thoughts indeed, but the truth of his words echoed in the sanctity of her heart.

For she felt the same. Had not every day since she met Guy Partridge been measured by whether she saw him or not? Did not her mind tend toward him at all hours of the day, even at the most inappropriate times?

Had she ever felt more loved, more safe, more desired, than when kissing him?

"There."

Isabella's gaze sharpened. "Where?"

"There," repeated Guy, his expression serious. "I saw it there, on your face, just for a moment. The realization that you loved me."

"No you didn't," said Isabella swiftly, raising her free hand to her face as though she could feel the expression he was describing.

He gave a wry smile. "Fine. You do not love me. In that case, I will take my leave."

Guy moved, descending a few branches, but he was forced to halt within a moment. At first, Isabella did not know why. Then she realized she had refused to release his hand.

His fingers and hers were still intertwined, and in this light, as something akin to desire yet stronger rushed through her veins, Isabella could not tell which were his and which were her own. Did it matter, as long as they were together?

"Isabella," breathed Guy.

An overpowering force of affection rushed through her, as though a dam had been lifted—as though she had been attempting to prevent herself from this place of intimacy and vulnerability, but the thought of losing him, of Guy leaving, was enough to break it down.

For she did love him. At least, if love was affection, and desire, and a need to be together, and pride in who he was, then was this not love?

"Guy," she whispered.

He knew what she needed immediately, without her saying a word. Standing upright on his branch, Guy brought his face to hers, and Isabella kissed him hard, eagerly, desperately, as though she had never wanted anything so much. Needed him. Craved him.

The kiss was searing, a brand upon her lips, and Isabella tilted her head to let him in, welcoming in his devasting tongue. She moaned as he grasped her shoulders, holding her close, and only when a freezing breeze rushed past did she pull away.

"Guy," Isabella said. "I...I love you."

The relief, the ecstasy on his face was complete—but as the breeze rushed through them again, Guy said nothing.

What he did, however, was most surprising. Isabella was forced to rise from the window seat and take a few steps back as Guy hitched up a leg and half clambered, half fell into her bedchamber. Before she could say a word, he had pulled down the window and prevented the breeze from reaching them.

Isabella stared as Guy straightened up. He was so much taller than she remembered, but, of course, for most of their...call it acquaintance, she was, well, sitting down.

Heat seared her cheeks, but she pushed aside the thought. Guy Partridge was in her bedchamber. The man she loved, who loved her, who had made declarations the likes of which she never thought she would hear.

And no one else was this end of the corridor, were they? She was surrounded by guest bedchambers, ready and waiting to be filled tomorrow. But tonight…

"Oh Guy," Isabella whispered, stepping toward him.

Being pulled into his arms was like coming home. It was everything she wanted: his strong arms around her, his powerful chest before her, her lungs filled with his scent, his lips on hers, and Isabella knew she could lose herself here, drowning in everything Guy was…

When the kiss finally ended, they were both a little short of breath, and Guy's lips were slightly bruised from their ardor. "Isabella."

"Guy," she said, nervously smiling.

There was only one direction this could go, that she knew, and Isabella welcomed it as she had welcomed him into her arms in the carriage.

They were going to make love. This would be the first time of many, of course, and when they were married—

"I need to tell you something."

Isabella smiled. She did not need to hear the specific words, of course; she knew precisely what he meant. He wished to ask for her hand in matrimony. Well, was that not obvious? Was she not about to give herself, freely and utterly, to him?

"Guy—"

"No, Isabella, I mean it," he said, pushing her away as she leaned up for another kiss. "Here, let's sit on your bed."

He moved to her bed, sitting at one end, and patted the spot beside him.

A rush of desire coursed through Isabella before pooling between her legs. She knew precisely what he could give her, how much pleasure. This was only the beginning.

But when she sat beside him, anticipation tingling across her skin, Isabella was astonished to hear no words of affection, but something rather different.

"I think it only right for you to know… Damn it all, I wish I had never… Isabella."

Isabella blinked. Why did Guy suddenly look so serious? "Guy."

He groaned. "Why is it so hard to think when you are looking at me like that?"

"Perhaps because you know I am about to do this," whispered Isabella.

Filled with passion, with boldness she knew came from their mutual understanding, she leaned forward and kissed his neck.

The sound Guy gave was something like a moan and sweet ecstasy, and it spurred Isabella onward; she reached for his cravat, attempting to untie—

"No, really, I must speak with you," said Guy, pulling away from her and moving farther up the bed, away from her eager hands.

Isabella sighed, her shoulders slumping. She would never have believed it would be this difficult to get Guy out of his clothes, for all his talk about being in love with her. "Then speak."

It was only when she focused on him that she saw he looked rather uncomfortable.

"Guy?"

"I am a sharker."

She blinked. She must have misheard. A "sharker"? What did he mean by it?

Guy groaned. "You don't even know what I'm telling you, do you?"

"Whatever it is, I am sure it is not important," said Isabella, reaching for him again.

It was most difficult to have Guy so close to her and yet so far away—and on her bed, too. She shivered. Oh, the pleasure they would share...

"A sharker, Isabella, is a man who tricks others out of their money."

Isabella stared. "I—I beg your pardon?"

Guy's face was a picture of agony. "Oh, it all started off so simple. I spoke the truth, Isabella, when I told you at Lord Jellicoe's that my father had fallen on hard times and it was my responsibility to keep my family above water...but as a trickster, a liar. Not quite a thief, but I am rather good at separating people from their money."

Isabella stared. The words were coming out of his mouth, and each of them individually made sense...but together, she could not fathom why he was saying such a thing.

Guy—her Guy, a trickster?

But he was a gentleman! He had been at Lord Jellicoe's for dinner, he was elegantly dressed, and though he kissed like the devil, there was nothing to suggest...

Isabella's mind returned to how they had first met. "Were you...you weren't actually attacked in that lane in Bath, were you?"

Guy smiled wryly, a little sheepishness in his eyes. "I was, as a matter of fact. Look, it has been years since I have—I am a gentleman now. I have built enough of a fortune to—"

"The lane," cut in Isabella.

She could hardly take in what she felt. Hot, certainly, and confused, and the desire was still there...but a liar? A thief? A criminal—that was what he was saying.

Trust her to fall in love with a man who couldn't keep on the right side of the law. Olivia had married a lord. Kitty had married the fifth son of a duke.

And she? She was in love with a sharker.

"I made some enemies in my youth, one of whom was the man you saw that day," said Guy, his face a picture of desperate innocence. "That part of my life is behind me, Isabella, you must believe me, but as you can see—"

"Not everyone is so quick to forget," said Isabella dryly.

Her mind whirred as she desperately attempted to take in what he was saying.

So. Guy Partridge was not a gentleman—not in the strictest sense of the word, anyway, even if he had stolen enough money to set himself up as one.

"I thought of myself as a sort of…well, a Robin Hood."

She looked up and saw pain on Guy's face. "You did?"

He nodded. "I only ever stole what someone could afford, and I shared the winnings with the poor in my area—why do you think Lord Jellicoe has such a fine opinion of me?"

Isabella laughed. Now it was all starting to make sense.

"You must believe me," said Guy quietly. "I am not that man anymore. I am respectable, in name and honor."

"And you haven't stolen from me yet," she said.

He looked hurt before seeing she was joking. "You don't steal from those you love."

Isabella tried desperately to hear her heart, but it was impossible. She loved him; she did not understand him. She had never lived in poverty, could not countenance stealing.

It was all so tangled.

"Isabella?"

She looked up. Guy looked uncertain; his smile twisted on his face as he attempted to read her expression.

"Consider me as just a man, please," he said quietly. "A man in your pear tree."

Isabella snorted. "A Partridge in a pear tree."

Guy looked around in panic. "Not too loudly!"

But she could not help it. Oh, she had never expected matrimony, love, passion in the first place, and now to discover it with a man who could touch her like that, who had a criminal past, who by his own admission adored her…

"Isabella!"

"Oh, there's no one this side of the house," said Isabella with a grin she hoped appeared as wicked as she felt. "We can be as loud as we want."

A glint of something dark and passionate flashed in Guy's eyes. "We can?"

She nodded, clambering onto the bed and crawling toward him slowly, heart in her mouth. Isabella did not know what had possessed her to be so forward, so wanton, except that she wanted him. Wanted all of him.

He had given her a taste of pleasure, not just once. Now it was time to share it.

"B-but my past," spluttered Guy as she pushed him onto the bed. "You don't care?"

"I certainly wouldn't want you engaging in any of that sort of activity again," she said, heart pounding as she sank into his arms. "But you'll have far more important things to worry about."

Guy's eyes were wide. "I will?"

Isabella nodded. "Like how to keep me satisfied, for example."

Her heart fluttered painfully as she spoke. Would he think her too forward? Would he be surprised, perhaps repulsed at her brazenness?

But Guy's expression of confusion had disappeared, replaced with nothing but desire.

"Isabella Fitzroy," he growled, twisting to turn her over so she was lying on the bed looking up at him. "I will make it my duty to ensure you are never left unsatisfied."

With that, he kissed her, and Isabella welcomed it, welcomed the fire and the fury, knowing she could never have him close enough. His chest pressed up against her breasts, and both of their breathing started to become jagged as they attempted to give and receive as much pleasure as possible.

"Oh, Isabella," Guy said, releasing her lips only to dip his head to her breasts.

Isabella moaned at the heady sensation of his lips dancing along her décolletage. Was this what it was to give up everything, to give in to every wild desire? Certainly, desire was throbbing between her legs, her body demanded release, and before she knew what she was doing, she spoke.

"Touch me."

Guy halted his kisses, lifting his head to meet her eyes. "I am touching—"

"No, I mean, between my legs." Isabella panted, clutching at his shoulders, eager to feel him again. "Please, Guy."

Not waiting for an answer, she took his hand and pulled it down, past her breasts, past her stomach, and to her thighs. Isabella scrabbled at her skirts, pulling them up, past her knee, and, without thinking, only feeling, placed his hand underneath her underclothes and right on her secret place.

They both moaned at the intimate contact. Isabella arched her back to welcome him.

"God, you're so wet," said Guy, immediately splaying his hand in her curls, arching one finger into her wetness.

"Touch me," begged Isabella, unable to help herself.

She needed him, wanted him, desperately wished to feel every inch of him, and she knew she could not hold off much longer, knew her body was calling out for him, and this was the only way she knew how to relieve this tension building in her—

"Ask, and I will obey," murmured Guy, kissing her neck as his fingers started to build a rhythm within her. "Damn, Isabella, you feel so—"

"Yes, yes, more," said Isabella, hardly able to take in a word he was saying.

Her whole body was focused on one point, the point between her legs that was being teased, touched, stroked, and the pleasure was building within her, building, building, and at any moment—

Her cry of ecstasy was muffled immediately by Guy's lips, and Isabella gave herself up to it, safe in the knowledge no one would hear her. Her body rocked, ripples of pleasure shook her limbs as the pleasure overwhelmed her, and it was only when the waves disappeared that she was able to open her eyes again.

There was a very odd look on Guy's face. It was one she had never seen before, and just before Isabella could say anything, he moved away.

"Guy?"

He was gone. Isabella's arms were empty, the loss of him complete, and she attempted to prop herself up on her elbows to see where he had gone.

Why would he leave her, in this moment, of all moments?

In the gloom, she saw him wrench off his boots and breeches. Isabella gasped at the heavy manhood standing erect between his thighs, and moaned with heady delight as Guy returned to the bed, pushed up her skirts, and settled himself between her legs.

"I need you, Isabella, and I need this," Guy said in a jagged voice. "I promise slow, sultry lovemaking later, but first—"

Isabella gasped. He had entered her; his manhood was inside her. They were more complete, more one than they had ever been before.

And it did not hurt. She did not know why she had such an idea it would be painful, to welcome a man inside her, but despite Guy's rather impressive bulk, he slid into her wetness as though she had been made for him.

As though they had been waiting for each other for eternity.

"Isabella," Guy said, "wait—Here."

Trying as best she could to concentrate when such heady delights were promised, Isabella allowed him to pull a pillow from the top of the bed and move it under her buttocks, raising her hips.

"What are you—"

"I'll go deeper," said Guy, eyes blazing. "And God, do I want deeper."

He thrust into her with his last word, and Isabella cried out with pleasure. Oh, the depth of him, the intensity of the move-ment, the friction he created, deeper than his fingers, stronger than his tongue—it was too much!

And yet not enough. Isabella looked up blearily, hardly aware what she was doing, but said only four words.

"Take off your clothes."

Guy did not need any more invitation. All his clothes fell to the bed, and Isabella gloried in the sight of him, the strange power there was in being fully clothed while a naked man thrust into her again, his face contorting as pleasure overtook them.

"I need to see you," Guy begged as he thrust again. "Isabella!"

Before she could say a word, Guy's hands had wrenched at her gown. The seams split and the material was torn away from her breasts. Her stays were pulled away with just as much strength, and Isabella gasped as her breasts were exposed to the air.

As Guy slid into her once again, starting to build a rhythm that Isabella knew all too well, he captured her nipple in his mouth, and she cried out—the pleasure was too exquisite.

"Guy, yes, yes," she said as flickers of sensual delight radiated from her breast now as well as her secret place. "Deeper, harder!"

It was wanton to speak in such a way, but Isabella did not care. She did not care about anything anymore, as long as she had Guy pleasuring her like this.

Because it was building. She knew it so well now, and yet it was so different, the way her body responded differently as Guy edged her closer and closer to ecstasy, and Isabella could do nothing but grasp his shoulders and cling on for dear life until—

"Guy!" Isabella moaned as her whole body spasmed with pleasure.

"Isabella!" Guy thrust into her twice, hard, and collapsed into her waiting arms.

CHAPTER NINE

WHEN ISABELLA OPENED her eyes, seeing December light falling past the curtain she had not closed in their haste last night, it was with a smile on her face.

Well. She would never have guessed at such things, such ways of pleasing, such ways of being pleasured.

"I'll go deeper. And God, do I want deeper."

The bed was warm, warmer than normal. But then, she had to expect that, did she not? With a man in it beside her.

Isabella rolled slowly over onto her side and smiled sleepily at the sight of Guy Partridge beside her. He was even more handsome asleep, if that was possible. All the cares of the world had disappeared, and he smiled as he dreamt.

"I promise slow, sultry lovemaking later, but first…"

Isabella's cheeks warmed, but not from shame. No, she could not feel shame for what they had shared together. Not after relishing pleasure in all its forms—at least, many of them. Guy had mentioned a few things they had simply not had the strength to try, things that made her body tingle now just thinking about them.

She had found him. Guy Partridge, the man she would love for the rest of her days—and with any luck, be loved by for almost all of them. The very thought of spending every night, and days too, with such delicate sensual delights, was rather astonishing.

Isabella had never believed such things could be found.

True, her sisters had muttered sometimes about delighting in the embraces of their husbands, but she had never wished to hear too much about that, and the more her sisters giggled, the more embarrassed she had become.

Not now. Not now she had tasted of Guy, knew what it was to tease each other until the early hours.

Isabella lifted her head and gently kissed him.

Guy's eyes fluttered open. "I will have you know," he said in a quiet voice, closing his eyes again, "I am not a morning person."

Isabella grinned. "Good. Neither am I, usually, but as it is near ten o'clock…"

His eyes opened. "Truly?"

She nodded.

Guy sat up in bed, then leaned against a pillow as he groaned. "By God, woman, you have completely exhausted me!"

"Good!" Isabella said with a laugh, moving into his arms and glorying in the way her skin tingled against his own. "I should think so!"

He kissed her head and tightened his embrace around her, and if Isabella was not mistaken, there was a rather hard morning welcome pressing against her hips.

"I don't know what you want me to do about that," she whispered, moving her hand slowly down to grasp his manhood.

Guy moaned as he kissed her neck. "Oh, I think you know very well…"

Isabella was astride him, guiding his manhood into her within a moment. There was slight tension within her, an ache from their amorous adventures, like a muscle that had been well stretched, but as Guy sat up and teasingly kissed her breasts, she felt herself stretch to welcome him in.

"Isabella…"

Their lovemaking was quiet, slow, tender. Isabella bit her lip as the pleasure overcome her, throwing back her head in disbelief at how glorious this was, and after Guy grunted as he thrust into her, the two of them fell back into the welcoming arms of the bed and each other.

"Now that," said Guy sleepily, pulling her close, "is how to transform me into a morning person."

Isabella giggled. "Anything for you."

"Anything for love," Guy murmured as he stroked her back. "You do know that you have completely stolen my heart, don't you?"

Hearing his words sparked such happiness within her that Isabella hardly knew what to do with herself. He loved her. She had his heart. He had given it willingly, of course, but she had also stolen it, taken it, demanded it with every fiber of her being.

"Good," she said, kissing his chest. "Does this mean you'll marry me?"

The words had slipped out from her mouth before she could stop them, but in truth, Isabella did not want to.

He brought out this side of her, this openness, this vulnerability she had never truly shared with anyone else. It was a marvel to discover this part of her that only responded to Guy's loving touch.

How much more did they have to discover together?

"My word, is that a proposal?"

Isabella smiled at the teasing lilt in Guy's voice. "More a threat."

"A threat?"

"There are five gentleman in this house who will not fear to call you out if you do not marry me," she said with a laugh. "Do not make me ask where my father keeps his pistols."

Guy groaned and kissed her head as he moved his hand lower, to her buttocks, clasping one of them and squeezing. "I thought I was the one here who was the criminal!"

"Oh, as if it would be such a hardship to be married to me," she said with a laugh, wiggling her bottom and delighting in the way Guy twitched. "Do you not think I can make you happy?"

"I think you make me very happy indeed," said Guy, caressing her buttocks.

"Guy!" Isabella moved to his other side, away from his questing hand, and propped herself up on her elbow to look seriously in his eyes. "You were not jesting last night, were you? You do truly love me?"

Guy's teasing smile disappeared at once, replaced by an earnest, devoted look. "More than anything. More than life itself, which appears may be a problem if your family discover me here."

Isabella smiled. It was rather rebellious, to think her family was probably downstairs for breakfast, or had already eaten and were going about their day…while she was in bed with a gentleman!

But he was perfect—perfect for her, arriving at just the perfect time. To think, if she had not taken that day trip to Bath, if she had not been able to escape Uncle Rupert and Aunt Frances, if she had not been trying to avoid that other gentleman and not wandered down that specific lane at that specific time…

"I think," she said quietly, "it might be time for you to do something far more dangerous than punch that man in the lane."

Guy's eyes widened. "You do?"

Isabella nodded, trying not to laugh. Oh, she was going to have so much fun teasing him—they were going to have so much fun together, exploring their bodies, glorying in each other's company…

"If you come down with me, I can pretend you have come to visit," she said thoughtfully. "It is Christmas, after all, and there will be many visitors paying their dues—"

A loud clattering outside the window halted her words. Both looked to the window.

"What on earth is that?"

Isabella smiled, rising from the bed and pulling a sheet around her. "I think I know very well what that is."

She was right. As she stood there, just hidden from sight by the pear tree, she saw multiple carriages slowly meandering up the drive.

Of course, it was Christmas Eve, the day that the rest of the Fitzroys were due here: the London Fitzroys, the Bath Fitzroys, the entire clan. Her mother would be going wild making sure that all the guest bedchambers were ready, and her father would be ordering gardeners to bring in enough winter foliage for the Christmas wreaths.

Isabella breathed in deeply. *Christmas.* It had felt like a very long December, but perhaps that was because the last week had been entirely absorbed by Guy.

He came up behind her and wrapped his arms around her. She moaned slightly. His naked body was warm even through the sheet.

"What's going on, then?" he whispered, kissing below her ear. "Are we being invaded?"

"Yes," said Isabella dryly, "though by my family, so I do not think we will be able to drive them out. Did I not mention all the Fitzroys are coming here for Christmas?"

Guy shook his head as he released her, turning her around. "All of them?"

It was hard not to smile. Isabella stepped toward the bed, releasing the sheet and seeing with pleasure what an instant reaction her naked body caused in her lover's face.

Moving swiftly to pull on her underclothes and stays, she said, "Yes, all of them. My three sisters, husbands, and children are already here—Olivia, Kitty, and Maria."

Guy sighed heavily. "I suppose you want me to put clothes on too."

"Not if you don't want to," said Isabella with a teasing grin.

"I had better put some on before I do something wicked. Go on, then, if your sisters and their families are here, who is arriving?"

Isabella pulled at the ribbon of her gown. "My uncle Rupert lives in Bath, and he has two daughters. Joy and Harmony, the younger married with a son."

Guy pulled up his breeches with a raised eyebrow. "Large family you have here."

"You haven't heard the half of it," she shot back with a laugh. "My uncle Arthur lives in London, and has six daughters, all told—all married save one."

Guy almost fell over as he tried to pull on a boot. "Six—six daughters?"

Isabella finished tying her gown with a flourish, and laughed as he stopped trying to balance and instead sat on the floor to pull on his last boot. "Jemima, Caroline, Esther, Lucy, Sophia…I'm forgetting someone."

"I think I'd forget too, with such a list—"

"Arabella," said Isabella. "There. All twelve of us Fitzroys, though, of course, nine of us are no longer Fitzroys at all, and Sophia won't be for long, if the family gossip is true."

"I hope before long you will be willing to give up that name."

She looked over at Guy, who was now fully dressed and leaning against the wall with a quizzical expression.

Delight—and a little relief—rushed into Isabella's heart. He would marry her, then. They would be together, they would happy—goodness knew where they would live, but it would be a place where happiness and pleasure would always be found.

"I will give it up in a heartbeat," she said softly.

Guy grinned. "Good. So long as we have that settled."

Isabella half wished she could stay up here with him, lock herself and Guy away for hours, days, where they only had to think about each other…but raucous laughter, the clattering of trunks, and chatter were echoing up the staircase upstairs.

The Fitzroys were all here.

"Christmas is our favorite time of year," Isabella said, stepping over to Guy and taking his hands in hers. "Would you… I mean, if you do not have anywhere else to—"

"As long as your mother can find me a bedchamber amongst the Fitzroy herd," said Guy quietly, "I would love to stay."

Isabella raised an eyebrow, her stomach twisting with pleasure as she spoke. "You do not wish to sleep here?"

He groaned. "Don't tempt me!"

Her heart beat rapidly as she and Guy left her bedchamber and walked along the corridor toward the stairs. How on earth was she going to explain his presence here? What if they did not like him?

How was she supposed to survive Christmas without his lovemaking?

"There she is!"

"Issy!"

"My word, who is that?"

Isabella smiled awkwardly. The entire Fitzroy family was in the hall, half of them still removing pelisses and greatcoats, more children than she knew what to do with rushing about, embracing cousins, teasing others, and being thoroughly spoiled by their grandparents.

But most eyes, in truth, were staring at her. Her and Guy.

Only then did she realize the one thing she had forgotten. Her hair. Her hair! Luscious and dark, it was still flowing down her shoulders in waves, unpinned and unrestrained.

Isabella caught Kitty's eye and smiled weakly. Her sister's face fell.

"No," Kitty whispered into the silence.

"What?" asked several cousins.

"I do not think we have had the pleasure of being introduced," said her brother-in-law Isaac at the bottom of the stairs.

"Ah, Mr. Partridge," said her mother as she put down a great-niece. "What an unexpected surprise!"

Isabella could not help it: she laughed as she took Guy's hand in hers and pulled him down the stairs as a cacophony of questions about who Mr. Partridge was and what he was doing holding hands with Isabella echoed around the hall.

All questions—at least, most—would be answered, and in time she was certain that they would all come to love him as she did.

But first of all…

"Is this the gentleman you were talking about?" asked Olivia as Isabella and Guy reached the bottom of the stairs.

Isabela swallowed and looked up at Guy, who grinned. "I should hope so!" he said.

"Guy!"

"Especially as she has just agreed to marry me," added Guy with a wink.

Gasps echoed around the room.

"Isabella, engaged!"

"You can have a double wedding with Sophia!"

"Thank goodness, I was beginning to worry—"

"Shush, think of Joy!"

Isabella's stomach turned. She had not thought of Joy. Against her better judgment, she looked over at her cousin Joy, who had struggled so much, she knew, with always being one of the unmarried Fitzroys.

And now she was the last.

But as Isabella focused, she saw a rather strange sight. There was Joy, as expected, looking just the same as she always did.

And yet not the same. Her hand was being clasped by a gentleman Isabella had never met. He had a wry smile on his face as he whispered something in Joy's ear.

Most intimately, too, now that she came to think of it.

"Is this a good time to introduce my betrothed, Gilbert Kitteridge?" said Joy in a shy voice most unlike her.

Isabella's mouth fell open, but she smiled as the three closest cousins to Joy—Sophia, Arabella, and Esther—descended on her in a wild embrace.

"Well, that's all of us," said Caroline wryly. "I do not suppose we will have any big celebrations from now on—except Christmas, of course."

"I…I would not be so sure of that."

There was so much noise and ruckus that for a moment,

Isabella was not entirely sure who had spoken. A few people near her turned round, looking for the speaker of such words, and a hush fell upon the hall as all faces turned to…Jemima.

Jemima, with red cheeks. Jemima, who had her husband Hugh's arm around her. Jemima, who was looking a little…well, puffy. It was not polite to say so, but Isabella could not help but think it.

Jemima, who had her hand clutched to her stomach…

"I did not wish to say anything for a little while, as w-we were not sure," she said in a rush, glancing up at her husband and smiling more boldly after receiving his encouraging nod. "But after six years of waiting…"

"You're not," breathed Isabella.

Jemima grinned, cheeks red now. "We are having a baby!"

It was Aunt Selina, Jemima's stepmother, who got there first, though several others also moved to embrace the Fitzroy cousin who had waited so long for this addition to their family. Aunt Frances was sobbing, sitting on a chair, utterly overcome, it appeared, by the good news, and even Isabella found herself blinking back tears.

"My word," came a quiet voice.

Isabella turned to see Guy with a broad smile on his face and a raised eyebrow.

"Your family never does things by halves, does it?"

Impulsively leaning up on her toes to kiss him—despite the scandalized gasp from her mother—Isabella shook her head with a laugh.

"Oh no," she said. "In the Fitzroy family, every Christmas must have a little scandal."

About Emily E K Murdoch

If you love falling in love, then you've come to the right place.

I am a historian and writer and have a varied career to date: from examining medieval manuscripts to designing museum exhibitions, to working as a researcher for the BBC to working for the National Trust.

My books range from England 1050 to Texas 1848, and I can't wait for you to fall in love with my heroes and heroines!

Follow me on twitter and instagram @emilyekmurdoch, find me on facebook at facebook.com/theemilyekmurdoch, and read my blog at www.emilyekmurdoch.com.